Once a Scoundrel

The Secret Life of Scoundrels #4

Anna Harrington

This is a work of fiction. Names, characters, places, and incidents are either products of the writer's imagination or are used fictitiously and are not to be construed as real. Any resemblance to actual events, locales, organizations, or persons, living or dead, is entirely coincidental.

Once a Scoundrel
Copyright © 2016 by Anna Harrington
ISBN-13: 978-1542548083
ISBN-10: 154254808X

ALL RIGHTS RESERVED.

No part of this work may be used, reproduced, or transmitted in any form or by any means, electronic or mechanical, without prior permission in writing from the publisher, except in the case of brief quotations embodied in critical articles or reviews.

NYLA Publishing
350 7th Avenue, Suite 2003, NY 10001, New York.
http://www.nyliterary.com

Dedication

Dedicated to my sister Denise for playing our own cutthroat games when we were kids. (Miniature golf will never be the same again.)

A very special thank you to Natanya Wheeler for helping with the publication of this novella, Sarah Younger for your patience with me, and the NYLA interns for your wonderful feedback.

And to Allison Fetters, for being such a wonderful friend and copy editor.

Chapter One

Hartsfield Park, Kent
September 1842

"I heard he had an affair with Baroness Marston."

Faith Westover rolled her eyes. If she had to hear one more giggling comment from her friends about Stephen Crenshaw, Marquess of Dunwich, she was going to scream.

As she did her best to ignore the group of silly things gathered near her and glanced around the crowded ballroom at the partygoers who had come to celebrate her father's birthday, she supposed she couldn't blame them. There was a decided lack of excitement at the party and a veritable dearth of interesting men, which she blamed entirely on her brother James for remaining at university. Which meant that none of his Cambridge friends were in attendance. Which meant that she and her friends had precious few eligible gentlemen to dance with.

And *that* meant that her friends had little else to occupy their attentions except for Stephen Crenshaw. Yet her friends weren't alone. The room buzzed with guarded whispers about the young marquess. Rumors had spread fast and thick all season about what Stephen had been up to since returning from India three months ago, but even though the partygoers were titillated by the thought of finally seeing for themselves the prodigal marquess, they knew not to openly disparage the man. Not at Hartsfield Park. Not when her father had been best friends with Stephen's father and uncle since their army days. But rumors still spread in whispers behind flitting fans and over glasses of wine about Stephen. Apparently, *that* was perfectly fine.

Although she was born into their midst, Faith feared she would never understand English society.

"No, it was Viscountess Rathbourne," another friend corrected amid a flitting of fans as all six girls leaned in to hear.

"It was the *dowager* Baroness Marston—"

"But isn't the dowager dead?"

"Yes," Faith answered with a heavy sigh of exasperation. "And it wasn't her daughter-in-law either, as the baron and baroness have been on the continent since

April."

"So it *was* the viscountess!" Her friend's eyes lit up. "What's the truth, Faith? You know him."

Had her friends lost their minds? "I don't know about a—" She lowered her voice and whispered behind her fan, "A man's *bed sport.*"

From the looks her friends gave her, none of them believed her. Instead, they all stared at her, waiting expectantly for her to declare the rumors true.

"Viscountess Rathbourne already has a...*friend,* in that regard," Faith confided. Oh, her mother would skin her alive if she heard her talking about her guests like this! But she was certain she wasn't the only one gossiping about Lady Rathbourne tonight, who was in attendance only because her husband served on the same committees in parliament as Faith's father. "And he isn't Stephen Crenshaw." Although the rascal would most likely be sorely put out that he wasn't, given the viscountess's famous beauty and infamous allure.

Disappointment darkened their faces, and this time, they flitted their fans with consternation that the juiciest of the night's gossip had been quashed so easily.

"All I can say for certain is that he accepted Mama's invitation to the house party." Which had been the only society invitation he'd accepted since his return. Given that he'd shadowed the end of the season rather than engaged in

3

it, Faith easily understood why so much gossip had arisen so quickly about him. All of it shocking. Truly, it was as if he'd returned to England and situated himself right back into the same flurry of rumors that had been swirling around him when he left.

Now he was due to arrive at any hour. He should have been here already, in fact, with the other guests who'd arrived that afternoon. But leave it to Stephen to flaunt even the most basic rules of society.

And truly, Faith didn't care if the scoundrel never appeared. She'd be glad of it, in fact. Glad! Then she wouldn't have to pretend as if they were still old friends, as if she were happy to see him again. As if a part of her didn't still blame him for leaving.

"Perhaps he decided to spend the sennight with his mistress."

Faith froze, her fan in mid-flit as an unexpected bolt of jealousy struck her. Her friend smiled, oblivious to the emotions roiling inside her and happy to broach the most scandalous of the rumors which had surrounded Stephen like a storm cloud since June. That he'd been keeping a mistress.

"I don't...I don't..." Faith stammered, unable to form an answer while her friends continued to stare expectantly at her as if she were the Oracle of Delphi, able to solve the deepest mysteries of the age. Of which Stephen Crenshaw had apparently become one.

Worse, she was unable to dissemble—all right, flat out *lie*—on his behalf because she'd not seen him since his return.

"How can you stand it?" one of her friends demanded. "I'm practically beside myself to see the marquess! Aren't you the least bit excited?"

"No."

"Oh, Faith!" Her friends turned up their noses in disbelief that she wasn't over the moon the way they all were at Stephen's impending arrival.

But that was because, unlike her friends, she knew him. And his recent behavior was simply Stephen behaving true to form by doing absolutely nothing to dissuade the busybodies and everything to make the rumors as scintillating as possible. He took a perverse pleasure in being the scapegrace the gossips proclaimed him to be.

Oh, he'd always been one for trouble. Even as a boy he'd resisted the responsibility and sense of duty that had been thrust on him since the day he was born a marquess. He wasn't spoiled the way so many young lords were—far from it. If anything, Stephen had been constantly reminded of how fortunate he was, expected to work twice as hard as his friends, and taught to behave like an adult from the time he was just a boy.

Under that stress, could anyone blame him for rebelling? So he'd secretly joined the army when he no longer found escape in cards, drink, and whatever other mischief he could find—including bedding the bored wives of half the queen's council, if rumors could be believed. Knowing what Stephen had been like during his university days, *that* rumor Faith was willing to accept at face value. In the ranks, he'd been just another captain, and he'd enjoyed his new-found anonymity, until his commanding officers discovered that he was the adopted son of General Nathaniel Grey, one of the most respected men in the War Office.

"You and the marquess spent a great deal of time together, didn't you?" another friend pressed. "Before he went off to India?"

"I suppose so," Faith dodged, turning her attention back to the crush around them before they could see any unbidden emotions for Stephen flitting on her face.

Because they had spent time together. As much as allowed, that is, because she had been just nineteen and in her second season, and Stephen had already earned himself a notorious reputation. But her older twin sisters had been in their fourth—and what would prove to be their last—season as eligible ladies before they married, with her younger sister Margaret in her first. The twins had taken

London by storm, much to their mother's joy and their father's chagrin, and Margaret had been all caught up in the excitement of her debut. With those three stealing attention everywhere they went and James finishing his last year at Eton, no one had paid Faith any mind...except for Stephen.

He and Daniel Llewellyn, his best friend from university, had come to London that May when they were graduated. Even then, rumors about Stephen's scandalous activities were swirling through Mayfair, and Daniel's penchant for engaging in the same sort of behaviors, surely egged on by Stephen, hadn't helped quell the gossip. He was a rogue, a friend...

And then somehow, he became more.

At first, she'd ignored his attentions. This was *Stephen*, after all. Someone she'd known all her life, a young man who oozed charm and flattery with every breath. Flirtation was his second nature.

Then he'd kissed her.

Oh, she was certain it had been a mistake. That Stephen Crenshaw would find her attractive...ridiculous! Then he'd done it again the next time they were alone, and again and again...Faith's head had spun to know that he wanted to spend time with her, and her heart— Oh, that silly thing simply somersaulted! He made her feel special and beautiful, as if she were an alluring woman instead of just another eligible miss in pastel satins. As if she were the catch of the season instead of the young lady he'd previously spent his existence ignoring.

Yet for all his kisses, he never asked Papa for permission to court her, and he never made her any promises of love. He also did nothing to curtail the rumors of scandalous trysts with society wives and widows.

At the time, she'd been too enamored of him to doubt his motivations. Now, though, she knew he'd only enjoyed the convenience of her kisses and the flattery to his pride of having her starry-eyed attentions on him. Nothing more. He'd been his scoundrel self, while she'd been too inexperienced with men to understand that.

Then in July, he and Daniel joined the army and left for India. Without warning or explanation to his family—without even a note to her. Whatever feelings she thought he had for her sailed away with him.

She'd been devastated and cried inconsolably, and all of it had been made worse in that she couldn't tell anyone. Not even her own sisters. They would have said it was her own fault for falling for a rake, and for *that* rake in particular.

And truly, wasn't it? She'd been a fool for ever dreaming of his love.

"Stephen was with Daniel Llewellyn when he was

killed, wasn't he?"

Faith stiffened at the unexpected comment. "Yes," she answered quietly.

"India must have been ghastly for him!"

She was certain it was. Especially since Stephen had given the order which led to Daniel's death.

Their regiment had been attacked, the order for a counterattack given...Daniel had been killed in the fray. There had been nothing Stephen could do to save him. Letters from Stephen had been few and far between before that; afterward, no letters came at all.

The next she'd heard of him was three months ago when Stephen had returned to London as unexpectedly as when he'd left. Three months during which he hadn't bothered to call on her while the rumors of his new rakish pursuits flourished. If she needed any more proof that she'd meant nothing to him, that was it.

"He'll need to find a wife soon," another friend interjected. "After all, he needs an heir."

Faith rolled her eyes. Oh for heaven's sake! Were her friends incapable of talking about anything except Stephen Crenshaw?

A commotion went up from the front entrance, and Faith caught her breath.

Speak of the devil...

Stephen appeared in the wide doorway. He paused to sweep his gaze around the ballroom and to unwittingly give English society their first good look at him in four years. Every inch of his regal demeanor declared him the marquess he was born being, and the devil-may-care grin, which even now crooked up his lips in an audacious half-smile, acknowledged the rakehell he'd become. Tall and broad-shouldered, with sharp cheekbones and piercing blue eyes, he commanded the room's attention with his quiet presence. Even though he'd arrived unannounced, everyone knew who he was, and a new round of whispers went up.

The Master of Ceremonies called out the next dance, and the orchestra struck up the first notes. But no one noticed. Their attentions were rapt on the marquess.

"Lady Faith, our dance."

Except for one, apparently.

She tore her gaze away from Stephen as Arthur Billingsby appeared at her side. Heavens, she'd completely forgotten that she'd agreed to dance with the man. He was a friend of her brother-in-law, which had made it impossible for her to turn him down.

Although dancing was the last thing she wanted to do at that moment, she knew her place at tonight's party and forced a smile. "Of course."

He placed her hand on his arm and led her onto the

floor. The couples took their positions, then bowed and curtsied before launching into a series of turns and sashays.

As she worked her way down the row toward the head of the line, not missing a step in her bobs and turns, Faith took surreptitious glances at Stephen. She watched from the corner of her eye as he crossed the room to greet her mother and father and then greeted his aunt and uncle, the Duke and Duchess of Chatham, before finally turning to his own parents. He shook the general's hand and lowered his head to allow his mother to kiss his cheek. When Lady Emily fussed over the way his valet had knotted his snow-white cravat in the latest minimalist fashion, Faith fought back a smile at his expense. Mothers never changed, no matter how old or troublesome their sons.

He'd certainly changed in appearance, though.

Despite being dressed in the same black and white formal attire as every other man in the room, right down to the black tailcoat worn open to reveal the intricately embroidered silk waistcoat beneath, nothing about him was ordinary. As if to impress that point, he'd forgone proper shoes for a pair of well-worn boots. They were the only indication in his apparel that he'd spent the last four years on horseback in the army rather than haunting the clubs on St. James's Street, yet no one could overlook the proud and straight-spined military bearing he wore like a uniform. A demeanor that distinguished him from every other young man in the room. His boyish features were gone, and in their place was solid man. Only those deep blue eyes, the curly black hair he still wore unfashionably long, and that charming half-grin that curled at his lips were the same.

Oh, how she remembered that grin! Faith had always found Stephen dashing and his scandalous nature secretly thrilling, even when she'd been a girl in the schoolroom and he'd been at Harrow. All those years when she stared after him dreamily while he'd paid her as much mind as a chair, she'd hoped that someday he might notice her as something other than Strathmore's daughter. That he might finally do more than make her stare after him longingly and sigh whenever he gave her the smallest compliment. That he might dare to kiss her in some dark garden the way he was rumored to do with other ladies...

Then he did.

And now her foolish heart regretted *ever* wanting that.

The dance ended. The ladies twirled back into their original positions as the last notes died away. Billingsby led her off the dance floor, taking the long way around the room to return her to her friends. And the way furthest from Stephen so she couldn't get a better look at him, not even when she craned her neck. *Not* that she wanted to see him anyway. He meant absolutely nothing to her now, she told herself. And someday she hoped to believe that.

"Dunwich's arrival has created quite a stir," Billingsby commented.

"As always," she muttered, the familiar anger at Stephen tightening her chest.

When Billingsby glanced down at her, puzzled at her tone, she forced a smile. After all, he was a friend of the family, so she needed to be polite to him, and he was only here for the evening. Thank goodness. Because she didn't like the way he kept staring at her chest. As if a giant stain covered her bodice.

"Your family is close to his, I understand," he added.

"Very." Although she wished with all her heart that they weren't. Then she wouldn't have to see Stephen again or speak to him...or pretend he hadn't wounded her.

"I'm certain you've heard the latest rumor, then."

Her smile faded. "You mean the untruth that he's keeping a mistress?" Surely Billingsby realized what a boor he was to spread gossip about a family friend to her face.

"Not just keeping her—"

She sniffed haughtily. No, apparently the man had no sense of decorum.

"—but her *and* her son, whom he refuses to acknowledge as his."

Her heart skipped. An *illegitimate* son? Impossible. Even from a scoundrel like Stephen. "You are mistaken, sir."

"Then so is half of London." He seemed amused at her defense of the marquess—heaven knew Faith was puzzled over it herself—but he didn't notice that she'd put as much room between them as possible in the crush while still holding onto his arm. By her fingertips. "You know as well as I how rumors start. There's always a grain of truth at the heart of each."

"Then *that* rumor is the exception." Her chest tightened until each hard beat of her heart made it difficult to breath. How on earth had she managed to find herself defending Stephen, the very last man she should be championing? "Dunwich is a peer who has given the last four years of his life in service to his country."

"Of course," he said quickly, as if finally realizing that he'd overstepped. "I didn't mean to upset you."

"You didn't. I just—" The words choked around the knot in her throat.

Oh bother! She'd sworn to herself that she wouldn't let Stephen's presence at Hartsfield Park upset her. Yet her eyes stung with unshed tears, and she trembled. Not with sadness, but anger. At Stephen for the way he'd so cavalierly treated her...and at herself that she still let him distress her.

She pulled her hand away. "Excuse me. I—I need a

14

glass of punch."

"I'd be happy to fetch—"

She walked away before he could see the hot tears glistening in her eyes. And what a relief that for once he was left staring at her back instead of her bosom. Of course, if Grace's husband found out that she'd just cut the man, she'd never hear the end of it from her sister. At that moment, though, she couldn't care less.

With trembling fingers, she took a glass of punch from the refreshments table, then welcomed the relief when the drink washed away the knot in her throat and helped ease the pounding of her heart.

The orchestra sent up the opening flourishes of the next dance. A waltz.

She sighed gratefully. She seldom waltzed and so could safely remain at the side of the room, enjoying both her punch and the moment's respite to gather herself from—

"Good evening, Faith."

The glass slipped from her fingers.

A hand shot out and grabbed it before it could smash against the floor.

She whirled around, her mouth falling open. Her heart stopped. *Stephen.* For one pained moment as she stared at him the world froze around her.

She should have hated him, should have scratched his

eyes out, should have screamed! All these years, she'd thought about what she'd say to him when this moment came, what cutting remark she'd level on him, what sophisticated and urbane wit she'd unleash on him...

But now that he stood in front of her, in flesh and blood and gazing back at her with the same wary unease that swirled through her, she couldn't find any words through the riot of emotions inside her.

Then he reached past her to set down the glass, and the moment shattered. Her heart lurched to a start, and the rushing blood roared deafeningly in her ears.

"Hello, Stephen," she forced out. *Why did you simply leave, as if I meant nothing to you? Did you think of me at all while you were gone? Did you know that I loved you?* Thousands of questions swirled inside her. But too overwhelmed in the moment to put voice to one, she lifted her chin and accused instead, "You're late."

"Still better than never." He gave her that devil-may-care grin that had fluttered hearts across England...and broken hers. "I wouldn't dare miss Strathmore's birthday party. Or the chance to catch up with the Westovers and Mattesons." His gaze searched her face, just as uncertain as she about how they would go forward. "I missed you, Faith." He hesitated, carefully selecting his words. "I treated you badly before, and I've come to ask your forgiveness."

She struggled to breathe as his words shivered through her. *Tell him that you need to return to your friends, that your sisters have asked you to join them...Oh, tell him anything to make him stop looking at you like that!* "There's nothing to forgive." She forced a smile. "I'd forgotten about it completely, in fact."

His eyes narrowed briefly, as if he'd recognized that for the lie it was. He didn't believe her, but she didn't give a fig about what he believed. He'd never again get close enough to wound her.

Even now, with his nearness stirring up the anger she'd carried inside her for so long, she wasn't certain if she could ever offer forgiveness. But she knew her role for this party, knew she was supposed to smile and be pleasant, to show that the Westover family had accepted him back into the fold with open arms. So she whispered, unable to put full voice to the lie, "We're still best of friends."

He held out his hand. "Then how about a waltz for an old friend?" When she hesitated, he cajoled, "I've been away for four years, and my horse made for a lousy dance partner."

Panic churned inside her. No, not a dance. Certainly not a waltz! Being in his arms would be torture, even in the middle of a crowded dance floor.

So she seized on the only excuse she could— "Papa doesn't like for me to waltz."

"Strathmore finds waltzing too scandalous?" he asked, disbelieving.

"He finds waltzing too scandalous for his unmarried daughters," she corrected. Not entirely a lie.

"Even with me?"

"*Especially* with you."

He laughed easily. Faith was suddenly reminded of how close they'd once been, and an aching sense of loss knotted in her belly. They'd never have that again.

"I'm a soldier come home from the wars." He clucked his tongue with mocking disapproval. "Where's your loyalty to crown and country?"

With the weight of what seemed to be every pair of eyes in the room on her, she knew she couldn't refuse him. Not an old friend of the family. Not when the busybodies were simply salivating for any new bit of gossip about him.

She drew a deep breath to gather her resolve and offered him her hand. "Apparently, the same place as my pride," she muttered, then winced as soon as the too-earnest words slipped from her lips.

"Don't worry," he assured her with a chuckle as he led her toward the dance floor. "It all goes before a fall."

Before she could respond to that cryptic comment, he pulled her into his arms and whirled her into the waltz.

She'd expected him to be rusty after being away from

society for so long, but he danced expertly through the steps, fluidly twirling her around the floor. Each movement demonstrated his natural athleticism, and she followed easily, aware of the heat of his gloved hand on the small of her back and the strength of his fingers folded around hers.

"For someone who doesn't waltz," he commented, carefully keeping his voice guarded so other couples couldn't overhear, "you're quite good at it."

"I could say the same about you," she grudgingly acknowledged with a sniff.

That earned her a crooked grin. "I aim to please you, Faith."

She stiffened at the subtle flirtation. Drat her flip-flopping stomach! And drat him for being so charming, for being so...*him*. He'd always been able to flummox her with only a passing compliment. Apparently, some things never changed.

"Mama is thrilled to have you as our guest," she commented, swiftly changing topics. Best to keep the conversation away from flirtations and firmly on the painfully proper.

"I would never refuse an invitation from the duchess." He glanced across the room in their parents' direction, then looked down into her eyes as he turned her in the corner and led her back across the floor. "Or miss an opportunity to see you again."

She ignored the butterflies in her belly, knowing his words were only empty flattery. "How odd, because Hartsfield is only a short ride from Elmhurst Park, and you returned to England in June," she reminded him, an air of pique permeating her voice. "You're a bit late in paying a call to close family friends."

His smile faded. "I am, and for that I apologize. You know how much you mean to me." He squeezed her fingers and added quickly, "How much all the Westovers do. But I had business to attend to at Elmhurst Park that kept me away."

She didn't believe that. When had he ever cared about his estate? During the years he'd been gone—long before that, if truth be told—she'd heard rumors about the mismanagement there by a series of land agents he'd hired to care about the estate in his stead. But there was another rumor that had caught her attention..."I've heard that you've decided to resign your commission and remain in England."

"Don't sound so surprised," he half-muttered, gazing down into her eyes. "I do have a marquessate and responsibilities here, you know."

"Oh, I know that." She gave a pointed lift of her brow. "I'm just surprised that you do."

His expression hardened at her chastisement, then

softened into a grimace. "I suppose I deserve that."

Faith supposed he deserved a lot more for running away to join the army and leaving his family worried. Leaving *her*. And if the rumors about his having a mistress and illegitimate son were true, oh, how much more he deserved!

"I'll admit that in the past I've been a bit..."

"Inconsiderate?" she prompted, unable any longer to keep her anger at bay. If it were possible to cut a man while waltzing in his arms, this was it. "Selfish? Irresponsible? Callous for not considering your mother's worry, *all* of our worry—"

"Yes, all that," he wisely interrupted and twirled her through a tight circle before she could describe more of the concern and pain he'd left in his wake. "But I'm a different man now. I've come back to England to start over."

Ha! And tigers changed their stripes. "I don't—"

"Starting with you, Faith."

The sincerity in his voice startled her, so much that she tripped. He tightened his hold around her and expertly kept her upright in his arms and moving through the steps. Surprised, she stared into his eyes, her pulse beating so furiously that she feared he could feel it.

"Me?" she squeaked. And drat his eyes for glittering like that at her discomfort!

Except that what she felt when he gazed so earnestly into her eyes wasn't discomfort. Far from it. A warmth simmered low inside her, the comfort of an old friendship mixed with the familiar longing she'd always felt for him, and when he squeezed her fingers, an electric tingle shot up her arm to her breasts, pebbling her nipples beneath her bodice.

"But I meant nothing to you," she protested softly, somehow keeping her voice from breaking. "And I told you, I've forgotten all about it. There's nothing to forgive—"

"That's a damned lie if ever I heard one," he bit out.

She stopped dancing, too stunned to care that the other couples had to step around them or that a new round of whispers went up across the ballroom.

"I was an arse for leaving you the way I did," he explained ruefully, bitter anger aimed at himself, "without so much as an explanation."

"Yes," she agreed in a breathless whisper, "you *were* an arse."

Wisely ignoring that, he said instead, with remorse thickening his voice, "And for that you have a right to blame me."

She tried to pull her hand away, but he held tight to her fingers, refusing to release her. "It doesn't matter any—"

"I want your forgiveness, Faith. I will do anything to

have it." He sucked in an uneasy breath. "Can you at least make an attempt to forgive me?"

The sincerity on his face sliced into her, leaving a raw wound in her belly. "I don't know if I can...I don't know..." Fresh tears stung at her eyes, and her words choked.

"All I ask is that you try." He tenderly squeezed her fingers.

She gave a jerky nod. "I'll try." It was the most she could promise now, when her confused heart simply didn't know what to feel.

He took her back into position in his arms. They danced on silently for several more measures before he murmured, "You must have hated me."

Unable to answer that with the truth, she turned her face away. It wasn't hate that she'd felt for him. "Your parents must be thrilled to have you home," she dodged. "They missed you."

A knowing flicker registered deep in his midnight blue eyes at her rapid change of topic. "Mother is, of course. I'm not so certain about Father."

"He is, too," she asserted, although she knew how strained Stephen's relationship had been at times with his adopted father. She also suspected that General Grey was part of the reason Stephen had joined the army, so that he could prove himself in a way the general would appreciate.

Something else nagged at her, though...She drew a deep breath and charged ahead by asking, "Since you're already here, will you ask my father for permission to court Margaret?"

"Your sister?" He puzzled. "Why would I do that?"

"It's always been expected that you would marry one of Strathmore's daughters." But now that the twins were married and she'd failed at her chance with him...She shrugged. "She's the only one left."

He stared down at her with a peculiar look that she couldn't place. "I don't like to do the expected."

"Or the proper."

He frowned. "What do you mean by that?"

"That you've always prided yourself on being scandalous and stirring up trouble." And the bigger the trouble, the more he was thrilled by it.

"Not anymore," he said with conviction. "I'm a respectable man now."

She wished she could believe him. That would go a long way toward forgiveness.

And yet..."I've heard rumors that you're keeping a mistress." Throwing all caution to the wind, hoping that he really had changed and that the gossips were wrong— "And that you have an illegitimate son."

He stiffened. Only one missed step as he turned her

through the last circle indicated that her comment pricked him, yet no one watching from the crush would have noticed anything wrong at all.

"Don't tell me you believe those rumors?" he dodged, glancing away.

Her heart fell. He hadn't denied them. He'd simply side-stepped the topic and avoided admitting the truth. Which saddened her more than she wanted to admit.

Apparently, he hadn't changed at all.

"I know what you were like before, Stephen." And he'd been exactly the kind of man to sire an illegitimate child. "Since you've returned, you've done nothing to discourage—"

"Daniel," he bit out with a ferocity that startled her.

"Pardon?"

He hesitated, his lips parted as if to tell her— He shook his head, then pressed his mouth into a tight line as he looked away.

"Stephen?" she pressed, a sudden dread clenching her at the mix of raw emotions flitting across his face.

"Daniel's death changed everything," he said finally, quietly, yet Faith had the feeling that he'd wanted to say something else.

"Of course it did," she murmured. She might never forgive him for the way he treated her, but at that moment, her heart melted for him.

Her eyes stung at the reminder of that letter from two years ago in which he described the uprising, how his regiment had been attacked without warning, how everyone would have been killed if not for Stephen's order to charge. A charge which resulted in his best friend's death. She couldn't imagine the guilt he felt over that, or how much pain he still carried inside him.

"When you wrote about Daniel, you didn't say what happened to you." She swallowed hard. "What was that fight like for you?"

"Hell," he answered solemnly, offering nothing more.

The last notes of the waltz sounded. *Thank God.* Around them, the whirling couples came to a stop. She gratefully stepped back, although the loss of the heat and strength of being in his arms rushed over her so intensely that she shuddered.

As she curtsied and he bowed, he murmured, "Meet me on the terrace at midnight."

She nearly fell over in her surprise as she rose. "Pardon?"

"I need to speak with you alone." When she hesitated, he pressed, "Please, Faith. For an old friend."

An old friend. She blinked away the stinging in her eyes and reluctantly agreed. "All right."

Stephen took her arm to lead her to her parents who

were waiting at the side of the room. The false smile Faith fixed on her face told everyone how simply thrilled she was to have the marquess back in England, even though her heart was ready to throw him onto a packet to China.

He lowered his mouth to her ear. "I missed you, Faith."

"You did not," she returned, forcing her smile not to waver.

"So much more than you realize."

They reached her parents, and he bowed politely before excusing himself, muttering something about seeking out a cigar. He gave her a parting look that sent the butterflies in her belly fluttering anew. Quick anger at herself flared inside her. Even now, after all the anguish he'd caused her, he could still so easily unsettle her.

"So," her father drawled as he watched Stephen walk away, "Dunwich has returned."

"Yes," Faith answered, struck by how Papa had referred to him. She couldn't remember her father ever using Stephen's title before. He'd always been referred to as Grey's son. Or simply Stephen. Never before had Papa acknowledged that Stephen was not only a fully grown man but nearly his equal as a peer of the realm.

She wasn't certain he had changed, but his return

had certainly changed the way people thought about him.

Papa leaned down to ask her, "Did you enjoy your dance?"

"Yes." Not entirely a lie. There were moments when she'd enjoyed it a great deal. She bit her lip. "Are you upset that we waltzed?"

"Not at all. He's Grey's son and deserves our hospitality."

She quirked a dubious brow at that, not certain she believed him, yet she placed a kiss on his cheek just the same. "Thank you."

"But be careful with him, Faith," he warned, as always the overprotective father who had England's most eligible gentlemen quaking in their boots at the prospect of asking to court his daughters. "The army changes the men who serve in it. He isn't the same man you knew before."

She hoped he was right.

Chapter Two

Stephen propped a hip against the stone balustrade on the garden terrace and stared at the glowing tip of his cigar as he waited for Faith.

If anyone happened to see him here, nothing more would be presumed than that he'd stepped out to enjoy a cheroot in peace. They wouldn't have known that his hands were trembling or that his gut had twisted into knots. And good Lord, how hard his heart pounded! From the nervousness inside him, he would have thought he was waiting for his first assignation with a woman, that he'd never met dozens of woman privately on dark terraces before.

But then, he'd never met privately on a dark terrace with Faith. And tonight might very well change everything between them.

"Stephen?"

He turned at the sound of her voice, a faint smile at

his lips. When he saw her, she stole his breath away.

She stepped toward him from the shadows, the pale sage green of her dress showing silver in the soft moonlight and her strawberry blond hair upswept. Petite and graceful, she seemed not to glide across the stone so much as float, and her green eyes were bright even in the shadows. His chest clenched hard. Dear God, she looked like an angel. No—a ghost. The same apparition who'd been haunting him for years.

When he'd walked into the ballroom this evening, he hadn't been prepared for the mature woman she'd become. How graceful and gracious. How softly alluring. Oh, Faith had always been attractive in an uncommon sort of way, with those full lips of hers that should have been too big for her face and that pert little nose which was perpetually dotted with freckles. But now she'd become simply beautiful. To think of how close he'd come to never seeing her again, of never knowing the woman she'd become—

But that was why he was here. To set everything to rights, to the way it all should have been before he left and ruined it.

"Faith," he murmured as she stopped in front of him. "You look beautiful."

Instead of the embarrassed expression he expected, she frowned at the compliment. "Empty flattery won't work on me, Stephen."

"Empty flattery?" Is that what she thought? He'd never uttered a more honest statement in his life.

"That's how you always used to get your way," she reminded him, carefully keeping her distance in case anyone should happen upon them. But he couldn't help thinking ruefully that it was more than propriety that kept her away. "Especially with women."

"I've changed." He paused pointedly. "*Especially* with women."

From the way she stiffened, she didn't believe that, and clearly, he had a long way to go before he regained her trust. Realizing just how far bothered him more than he wanted to admit.

He dropped the cigar to the stone and crushed it out with the heel of his boot. "You used to like it when I paid you compliments."

She dismissingly shrugged her slender shoulders. "I used to think you meant them."

"I did. I still do." He fixed his gaze on hers in the shadows, hating that she no longer trusted him. "With you."

She laughed, a light sound that floated gently on the night air and pierced into his chest like a sword. "And I'm to believe that I'm somehow different from all the other women you flatter?"

"Yes."

Her green eyes studied him uncertainly in the shadows. He didn't blame her for being wary, knowing how he'd treated women before he left for India—how he'd treated *her* in particular. When he'd taken nearly as much thrill in the scandal of what he was rumored to have done and with whom than in the acts themselves. When he didn't care what women gained in their encounters as long as he found his own pleasures.

But he never would have intentionally hurt her.

"I've never once lied to you, Faith, in all the years we've known each other." It was important that she realized that. "And I promise you that I won't start now."

She shook her head with an impatient sigh, as if that heart-felt admission simply proved her correct on how he was willing say anything to get what he wanted. Her reaction galled him. "Why did you ask me out here, Stephen?"

"I need to talk to you." He hesitated. "About Daniel."

Even in the darkness, he saw her face pale, becoming ghostly white in the moonlight. "I told you," she whispered. "No one blames you for his death."

If only that were true. He constantly felt Daniel's death like a knife in his gut.

"And it was wrong of his parents to have made you

swear to keep him safe."

The knife twisted. "Faith, please listen—"

A couple laughed loudly as they stepped onto the terrace, followed by two more. The French doors stood open wide, letting in the cool air and the fragrance of night-blooming jasmine and inviting more party guests to spill out onto the terrace.

The last thing he needed for this conversation was an audience. He held out his hand. "Come down into the garden with me where we can talk in private."

Eyeing him apprehensively, as if he were the devil himself, she stepped back to put even more distance between them. Each step clawed at him. "I need to return inside. I'll be missed and—"

"Come down into the garden with me, Faith," he repeated, this time much more deliberately, wishing he could make her understand through sheer will the importance of what he wanted to tell her.

She froze, and a new wariness swept over her face. She parted her lips as if to say something, then shook her head and turned toward the house.

He grabbed her arm from behind and stopped her. For a moment, he half-expected her to yank free and slap him, at the very least to storm away—instead she stilled, every inch of her tensing like a coiled spring.

33

"Just down the steps to the edge of the lawn," he explained in a low voice at her ear. "Close enough to the house to be proper but where we can talk without being overheard." When she hesitated, he drew a deep breath. "You asked about those rumors, the ones which claim I have a mistress and a son. I want to tell you the truth."

She asked bluntly, "Have you placed that woman into one of your properties?"

"Yes," he admitted, not having a choice. That was easy enough to prove. All she had to do was check with anyone at Elmhurst Park to learn that Mary was living there.

"Then I don't need to know anything more."

When she started to walk away, he tightened his hold on her arm and held her in place. *Damnation.* They hadn't even started the discussion they needed to have, and already he was mangling this. Badly. He took a deep breath and tried again. "Her name is Mary Halstead, and I want to explain about her."

Refusing to look over her shoulder at him, her eyes gazing straight ahead, she said quietly, "The rumors say that she's the daughter of an East India official in Calcutta."

"She is." *Was.*

"That you met her in India."

"Yes." *So did Daniel.*

"And that you've given her money and clothing, established a household for her—"

"That's no one's business but mine," he interrupted. Those rumors, too, couldn't be denied.

A knowing flicker of betrayal darkened her face. "That sounds to me exactly how a man would refer to his mistress."

"She isn't my mistress!" he ground out, far too loudly, and drew the attention of the nearest couple, who sent them curious looks before moving further down the terrace.

"Then what is she to you?" she pressed.

He clenched his teeth at the distrust in her voice. "A good woman who doesn't deserve to be disparaged."

She turned her head to look at him. Accusation blazed in her eyes. "What is she to *you,* Stephen?"

Good Lord. Even Faith believed the gossip over his word. He'd come here to set everything to rights with her, but he didn't realize until that moment how hard it was going to be. "She's a friend in a difficult situation, nothing more."

She lowered her gaze and said quietly, "She has a child."

"Yes. His name is Jeremy." Anticipating her next question, he drawled, "He isn't mine."

She hesitated, as if to say something about the boy—

then shook her head instead. "It doesn't matter."

So much more than she realized. "The boy's father was a soldier in India," he continued carefully, dancing as close to the truth as he dared until he could gauge her reaction. Knowing Faith as he did, it was best to ease into it. "He was killed, and Mary was left with nothing. I made certain she had safe passage back to England and someone with her while she had the baby. They're living under my care at Elmhurst Park." He felt compelled to add, "Temporarily."

"But why would you do that? Surely, her own family would have taken her in, or her husband's family would—"

"She has no one but me," he bit out, once more chafed by the situation in which Mary had been thrust.

And him right along with her.

If not for Mary and Jeremy, he could have quietly returned to England. He could have started his new life with a clean slate and proven to everyone—*especially* to Faith— that he'd truly changed. That he was no longer a scapegrace but a respectable man. Instead, every step he took was an uphill battle.

This was his punishment, he supposed, for giving the order that killed Daniel.

Her shoulders sagged with obvious disbelief. "Isn't that the same story every compromised young lady makes these days? That her husband died in the army?"

"Do you have so little trust in me?" he pressed, irritated that she refused to believe him.

Her eyes flickered in the shadows. "You forget, Stephen. I knew you from before, when nothing you said or did could be trusted. When you certainly didn't keep company with virtuous women. Perhaps you should have been more like Daniel and stayed away from scandal."

He clenched his jaw in quick anger. The indictment on her face and the way she measured him unfairly, damning him before he even had the chance to prove himself—

"Well, too bad we can't all be like Daniel," he drawled bitterly.

Her spine stiffened, and she pulled her arm away. "What do you mean?"

Damnation. "Daniel fell in love with Mary," he admitted with a heavy breath, regretting his outburst. "Jeremy is Daniel's son."

*****

Faith stared at him as confusion whipped through her. What Stephen had said...*Impossible.* She didn't hear him correctly, *couldn't* have heard—

She repeated in a whisper, too surprised to speak any louder, "Daniel Llewellyn...is the father?"

When Stephen cursed quietly at himself, she knew it was true.

Disbelief sank through her. How could that be? True, Daniel had created quite a stir that last season, matching Stephen's roguish behavior measure for measure. But that had only been because of Stephen's bad influence...hadn't it? Daniel came from a respected family. Conservative Tories, no less. He never would have been so careless...would he?

"Let me explain." Stephen gestured toward the steps leading into the dark garden below. "Please."

She nodded stiffly. Bewilderment churned inside her as he led her down from the terrace to a stone bench at the edge of the gravel footpath encircling the lawn. In the shadows and with the privacy of the terrace's stone wall behind them, they remained close enough to the party not to raise any eyebrows yet far enough away that they couldn't be overheard.

She sat and looked up at him. "Daniel and that woman...How did it happen?"

He drew in a deep breath. "We'd been in India almost two years," he began haltingly, as if he didn't know where to start. "A few officers from our regiment were requested to travel to Calcutta to meet with officials from the East India

Company. I was selected, and Daniel came along as my aide-de-camp. One night, we were invited to a dance. They needed partners for all the Company wives and daughters." He paused, and she half-expected him to start pacing. "And Mary was there."

"That's when he met her?"

"Yes. I didn't know that something had sparked between them. He kept it secret from me for months." Then he *did* begin to pace the short distance in front of the bench, his boots crunching on the gravel. "He planned to wed her and use her father's influence to secure a position for himself within the Company."

"Did they marry?" Her mind raced as she tried to remember the few letters Stephen had sent, and there had been no mention of a wedding.

"No, they didn't," he said quietly, stopping still. "Because a few weeks later he was killed."

Her hands clenched the edge of the bench in grief. *That* letter she remembered all too well.

He drew a ragged breath and continued quietly, "A few months later, Mary arrived at the regiment, distraught and inconsolable." He paused, his face grim. "She was with child."

Her hand flew to her mouth. "Oh, that poor woman," she breathed softly through her fingers, her heart aching for her. "She must have been terrified."

He nodded. "She was. Her family had refused to help her and cut her off, and Daniel's family accused her of attempting to extort money from them, of smearing their dead son's name."

Knowing Daniel's family as she did, Faith readily believed that. The Llewellyns would never have tolerated a scandal.

"She had no money," he continued, racking his fingers through his already unruly hair, "nowhere to go, and no one to help her."

"Except you," she acknowledged softly. He'd been Mary's only salvation, keeping her from the streets or the poorhouse and her baby from the orphanage. *That* certainly wasn't the Stephen she'd known before. Oh, he would have felt pity for her situation, certainly, but he wouldn't have gone out of his way to help her.

He heaved out a hard breath. "Yes."

"That's why you haven't protested any of the rumors," she whispered, understanding dawning in her. "Because you were protecting her and Daniel."

He gave a jerky nod. Even in the shadows, his expression was dark, his shoulders heavy with responsibility.

She rose and stepped slowly toward him. "You did a wonderful thing."

"Did I?" The bitterness in his voice surprised her.

"Yes," she said with as much conviction as possible, laying a hand on his arm. "Because of you, she's safe, and her child has a chance for a good life."

"Living off my charity, uncertain of the future, the center of vicious gossip and rumors?" He stepped back to pull himself free from her touch and shook his head. "They're in this situation *because* of me." He hesitated only a heartbeat before confessing, "Because I killed Daniel."

Her chest tightened at the anguish flitting across his face. "That's not true."

"I gave the order to charge," he countered, his eyes somber.

She stared at him, for the first time clearly seeing how much guilt and remorse he carried inside him over Daniel's death. He'd wrongly blamed himself, and now he felt obligated to piece together the future that Daniel's death had shattered, even at the price of his own reputation. She said firmly, "You did *not* kill him, Stephen."

"I did. And I have spent the last two years coming to terms with that, struggling to understand why him." A haunted expression marred his handsome face. "Why me."

"It was a battle, and men die in battle," she insisted breathlessly. "It wasn't your fault."

He squeezed his eyes shut and nodded, as if trying to

accept that truth. But grief and guilt gripped him hard, and her heart melted for him.

For the first time since he'd left, she was able to let go of the anger she felt for him. In its place came forgiveness and a longing to comfort him.

Whispering his name, she lifted onto her tip-toes and rested her palm against his cheek in an attempt to reassure him. Every ounce of her wanted desperately to heal the wounds they both carried inside them. To finally let go of the past and move on.

"You have to forgive yourself," she murmured as she lowered herself away. "You *have* to..."

He pursued, cupping her face between his hands to keep her close. His mouth lowered to hers—

"Don't," she protested softly, turning her face away. She'd only wanted to ease his troubles, not encourage him to kiss her. Fresh pain blossomed inside her for him, for the torment he felt at Daniel's death...and for her own foolish heart, which pounded furiously for him despite knowing better.

He lifted his head and stared down at her, his dark eyes glowing with emotion. "I need this, Faith, more than you know," he admitted in a breathy whisper. "And so do you."

Slowly, he lowered his mouth again to kiss her.

She broke out of his hold and stepped back. Immediately she missed his warmth and strength, regretted the loss of the promise of his kisses. And the way he looked at her, his eyes afire, as if only a thread of restraint kept him from sweeping her into his arms and carrying her away into the dark garden—

He hadn't changed at all.

"You shouldn't try to kiss me like that," she whispered. Folding her arms across her chest to keep herself from reaching for him—or slapping him, she'd yet to decide which—she shook her head. "You had no right. And I don't want you to."

He quirked a dubious brow at her denial.

Frustration poured through her and burned in the unshed tears in her eyes. Oh, blast the devil!

"Faith?" Her mother's voice cut through the darkness as she approached through the shadows. She saw Stephen and stopped. "Dunwich," she said tightly, clearly displeased to find him arguing with her daughter in the shadows.

Stephen inclined his head. "Your Grace."

"I noticed that Faith had been gone from the party for some time, so I came looking for her." Her eyes moved between the two of them, although thankfully the shadows were too dark for her to see the hot blush on Faith's face. "Is everything all right?"

"I'm fine," Faith whispered. Her eyes stung, and she blinked hard to tamp down the fresh frustration and anger. How was it possible that Stephen could still hurt her after all these years?

"You are not fine." She took Faith's hand and leveled her gaze on Stephen, her spine straightening in that imperial bearing of hers that would have intimidated the queen. "Is there a reason you've upset my daughter?"

"It was nothing," Faith interjected before Stephen could answer. A stab of guilt at dissembling with Mama shot through her— "We were only talking, about India."

"We were talking about Daniel Llewellyn," Stephen corrected quietly.

"I see." Her mother's shoulders eased down. The hard gaze she'd given him softened sympathetically, and she linked her arm through Faith's. "Well, I think there has been enough talk for one evening. Why don't you come back inside with me, Faith? You can enjoy the dancing." She paused meaningfully, her gaze fixed on Stephen. "Dunwich, I am certain that you'd like to walk around the gardens for, say, twenty minutes or so?"

"Of course, Your Grace," he answered, the rake in him completely understanding the meaning behind her request.

With his gaze lingering softly on them, her mother led her back toward the house, mercifully not asking any questions about why she was lingering in the shadows with Stephen. Thank goodness. Because Faith had no idea how she would have answered them.

Chapter Three

What the devil was she up to?

Hours later, the ball having ended and the guests scattered, Stephen leaned on his forearms over the balustrade of the first-floor gallery above the front hall and watched through the dim shadows as Faith slinked silently toward the door. Still in her satin gown and slippers, her strawberry blonde hair pinned on top her head, she also wore a man's greatcoat that was so long it nearly reached her ankles.

A footman who was carrying down the last of the glasses from the billiards room hurried down the hall toward him. Stephen stopped him, then motioned for him to be quiet before gesturing downstairs.

He pulled a coin from his pocket and held it up. Bribery worked just as well among household servants as it did among soldiers. "Any idea where Lady Faith is going?"

The footman's lips curled as if the coin were the easiest one he'd ever earned. "There's a horse in the stables gone lame, sir," he answered quietly. "Lady Faith often sneaks out at night to tend to the animals."

He smiled wryly. Of course she did. The Duchess of Strathmore had tried to instill in her children a sense of charitable duty in helping the sick and poor by encouraging them to volunteer in London hospitals and assist the village doctors at their estates at Hartsfield and Brambly. But Faith had carried her medical knowledge into the barns and applied all she'd learned to lambs, foals, chicks, puppies, kittens...While her sisters had been bandaging a wounded horse guard, Faith had bandaged his horse.

Having a wife who wanted to be a leech drove Strathmore to distraction; having a daughter who wanted to work in the stables nearly undid the man.

Stephen tossed the coin to the footman, who took it and hurried on his way, then leaned over the railing, to once more gaze down at her. A strong urge to follow her rose inside him. He wanted to talk to her again. There was so much more that needed to be said—

But not tonight. She wasn't ready yet.

She'd agreed to try to forgive him and be friends again, and he let that be enough for now. *Friends.* His lips twisted at the irony. Yet it was a first step, and he had to choose carefully how to reveal the rest. But he had time, and India had taught him patience. After all, he'd already waited years; what were a few more days?

With a glance over her shoulder, not seeing him watching from the shadows above, Faith slipped out the door.

Tending a lame horse in a ball gown—that was just like her. Always unpredictable. Still a bit careless. Yet always a soft spot in her heart for poor creatures needing comfort.

He only hoped she possessed enough softness in her heart to comfort the poor creature he'd become.

Shoving away from the railing, he moved through the gallery and down the hall. The house was finally settling down, now with dawn only a few hours away. The guests who had come only for the dance had been spirited away by a long line of black carriages. Those who were remaining for the house party were tucked into bedrooms for the night, although not necessarily in their own rooms nor with their own spouses.

To think that four years ago he would have been among them—*Christ*. If he'd wanted nothing more than meaningless swiving tonight, he could have easily had it. The hungry looks Viscountess Rathbourne had been sending him all evening practically shouted how amenable the woman was to doing just that. For God's sake, she'd practically groped him in the garden when he'd stepped out for a moment of fresh air.

But he didn't want to go back to that life.

Although society expected him to take up right where he left off as a rogue who had filled his time doing nothing more productive than drinking himself into oblivion and gambling away his fortune, he had other plans. Too much had changed for him to ever go back. He'd seen too much violence and destruction, experienced too much brutality and pain. It had taken the death of his best friend to make him realize that life was both astonishingly short and unbelievably precious. That he'd done a damnably fine job so far of wasting it. And that it was time to set everything to rights.

He walked into the smoking room and found Strathmore, Chatham, and his father sitting in front of a fire which had already burned down to the coals, yet none of the three men were ready to turn in for the night. He helped himself to a glass of cognac from the side table, and all three sets of eyes flicked to him as he took a cigar from the humidor and lit it on the oil lamp. But their conversation over Prince Albert's undue influence on the queen—and the queen's undue influence on the prime minister—continued uninterrupted.

"She's having a child per year now," Edward

Westover, Duke of Strathmore, mused as he kicked his feet onto the fireplace fender yet somehow remained impossibly straight-spined in the crushed velvet chair. He was celebrating his fifty-fifth birthday this week, but the man still possessed a solid build maintained through hard work on his land.

Thomas Matteson, Duke of Chatham and Stephen's uncle, raised a brow. "You'd begrudge her a family?"

"No." Strathmore flicked the ash from his cigar. "Not as long as she doesn't begrudge us her role as sovereign."

"The colonel's stuck in his ways," his father informed Stephen as he sank into the empty chair beside the three men. "He still can't come to terms with the fact that the monarch married a German."

"God preserve us," Strathmore muttered and finished off his brandy in a gasping swallow. The two old friends beside him chuckled.

"The empire's changing, Edward, whether we like it or not," his father commented with a shake of his head. "Railways crossing the countryside, steam packets crossing the Channel...The old days are gone."

Chatham pointed his cigar at Stephen. "It's in the hands of men like Dunwich now."

Strathmore groaned. "Then God *truly* preserve us!"

Stephen's lips curled into a wry smile.

50

The duke pushed himself out of his chair and crossed the room for more brandy, fetching the entire bottle.

"So, Dunwich." Strathmore shot him a glance as he refilled his drink, then topped off Chatham's glass. "You're back in England." He set the bottle aside. "Is it for good this time?"

"Yes." Stephen studied the glowing tip of his cigar. "I've resigned my commission."

Strathmore slid a not-so-subtle glance at the general. "Your idea or your father's?"

"Mine." He clamped the cigar between his teeth and mumbled around it, "If the general had his way, I'd be in the cavalry for the next twenty years."

All four men knew that was only a slight exaggeration.

"Military service does a man good," his father defended himself.

"Indeed," Chatham seconded. "The hardest and best years of my life were spent fighting in Spain."

"Where you also chased Spanish flamenco dancers," Strathmore reminded him.

"And where we had to repeatedly rescue you from Spanish fathers and husbands," Grey added.

Chatham laughed, then he cleared his throat and pinned Stephen with a look. "No need to tell your aunt about any of that."

"Or my wife," Strathmore agreed.

"Or your mother," his father finished.

Stephen chuckled and took a sip of cognac. On that, his lips were sealed. Three stronger and more independent-minded women he'd never met than the two duchesses and his mother.

Except perhaps for Faith.

"What are your plans, then?" Strathmore pressed. "What will you do to occupy yourself?"

"I'm a land-owning peer," he reminded them as unassumingly as possible of the position he was born into, although he didn't blame them for forgetting. He'd only just come into his majority when he enlisted, and they'd known him before as nothing more than a reckless man-boy who lived his life on the edge of expulsion from university and under constant threat of being shot by a jealous husband. He'd certainly never given them cause to think of him as a responsible man. That was just another one of the many things he planned to change. "Parliament will take up half the year, and Elmhurst Park will occupy the rest." He wasn't fond of the estate. The old house was too silent for comfort, too still. But he had plans to change that, as well. "I'll have more than enough responsibility to fill my time."

Strathmore returned to his chair. His dark eyes fixed

on Stephen. "I've heard rumors about how you've been spending your time."

Stephen held his gaze. He'd known this fight was coming, which was one of the reasons he'd sought out the three men out tonight. The military had taught him that it was always better to be the one dictating the terms of battle. "You mean that nonsense about Mary Halstead."

Damn those rumors. And damn those old busybody hens who had nothing better to do than spread nasty untruths about the most vulnerable of people.

"She had to leave India unexpectedly," he explained, unwilling to go into more detail than that, but he was certain the three men knew why. "She had nowhere to go, so I let her stay in one of the cottages at Elmhurst. She'll be moved by next month." *If* his plans for his visit here went as he hoped.

Strathmore silently raised his glass to take a sip, yet his expression told Stephen that he didn't believe him.

But Stephen didn't argue further, knowing that any protest would only add toward his guilt. He was careful not to let any emotion show in front of the man who had raised him as if he were his own son and the two dukes who had been like second fathers to him. They were worried about him, but the devil take their interference.

"You should be careful, Stephen," his father put in,

concern in his voice. "A woman in Miss Halstead's position—"

"*Mrs.* Halstead," he corrected. A bald-faced lie. She wasn't married, but he'd be damned if he let anyone criticize her any more than necessary.

"A woman in her position," the general tried again, "especially if she has a son to raise, might see a wealthy peer as a path to fortune. She might do anything to gain your favor."

"Gentlemen, I appreciate your concern." Another lie. While they might have been worried, it sure as hell felt like meddling, and he damned well didn't appreciate it. "But I assure you that Mrs. Halstead doesn't view me as a path to anything."

Except to her ruin. He swallowed down half his cognac, but all the brandy in the world wouldn't erase his guilt.

"The rumors have it otherwise," Chatham drawled.

"I'm certain they do." He shoved himself out of the chair to relight his cigar. "The gossips will just have to be disappointed that they aren't true."

"Not that the truth will keep any of those old hens away from a juicy bit of *on dit*," Strathmore put in. "The more unbelievable and outlandish, the better, as far as they're concerned. They'd rather ruin you than see you vindicated."

"And in the meantime you might want to consider preventing more rumors," Chatham suggested. "Avoid gambling and drinking for a while, ease back into society—"

"Stay away from loose women," his father interjected with a pointed glance at him.

He paused in mid-puff to move his gaze between the three men. All his antics from before the army had already damned him in their eyes, but they were willing to give him a second chance. Only time would prove his worth to them.

"I fully intend to do just that," he affirmed solemnly, and meant every word.

His comment seemed to mollify the men's concerns, because he saw the shoulders of each relax as they sat back deeper into their chairs. Thank God. He admired and appreciated each of them, but having his father's expectations to live up to was bad enough. Throw in the two dukes...could anyone wonder why he'd joined the army to escape to India, to finally be able to prove himself on his own merits?

But India had done far more than just that. He hadn't lied to Faith. He *wasn't* the same man now that he was when he enlisted. Long stretches of boredom punctuated by moments of sheer terror and fury, the struggle to find enough resolve to care about civilians who might turn in a heartbeat and attempt to kill him, the cold unfamiliarity of everything around him...giving the order to charge that resulted in the death of his best friend. No one could go through that and return the same, nor could Stephen shrug off the responsibilities fate had given him as a result of that.

"Now that you're back in England," Chatham commented, tossing his cigar stub into the fire, "any plans to follow your father into the War Office?"

Stephen shook his head. He'd seen more than enough of the military for one lifetime. "I'm the last person the War Office would want among their ranks," he half-joked, returning to his chair. "Besides, I'd be nothing more than a poor imitation of the general."

His father smiled at the soft compliment, although he deserved far more praise than that. General Nathaniel Grey was one of the best men the War Office had ever produced, and his name was legendary, even among the soldiers in India. Which was why Stephen had enlisted secretly. The last thing he needed was for the general's shadow to fall over him all the way to Calcutta. It had taken a year for his relationship to the general to be revealed inside his regiment, but by then, he'd already proven himself to his men and to the other officers.

"Any plans to find a wife?" Strathmore asked.

"Good God, colonel!" Chatham looked aghast. "The man survived India. Are you trying to kill him off now?"

"Slowly and painfully, too," his father mumbled. Then he sent him a pointed glance. "Your mother doesn't need to know anything about this entire conversation."

Stephen grinned.

"Marriage isn't such a bad idea," Strathmore conceded. "If you're serious about taking a leadership position in parliament and an active role in overseeing your properties, then a wife would be helpful."

More than helpful. A wife might just save him.

He stared into his glass as he slowly stirred the brandy and admitted quietly, "Actually, I've been considering doing exactly that."

All three men gaped at him with open surprise.

"Don't look so stunned, gentlemen." *Christ.* They were staring at him as if he'd just admitted to stealing the crown jewels. "I'm twenty-six." With a title and more land than he knew what to do with, more money in the bank than he could count, a need for an heir..."It's time I focused on the marquessate."

More than that, it was time he focused on securing that which was most important to him. On finding a purpose. A true future. Finally healing all the misery he'd caused. He wouldn't stop until he had everything he wanted, including the one thing a rogue like him was never supposed to have.

He wanted Faith.

Chapter Four

Beneath the afternoon sunshine, Faith removed her bonnet and dangled it by its ties at her side as she ambled down the lane.

Oh, how glad she was that she'd decided to go for a walk! This was so much better than staying inside the house with the ladies, doing needlework or watercolors. She also didn't think she'd be able to tolerate the fresh gossip that was certain to arise among them, especially with the men spending the day away fishing.

She deeply breathed in the fresh air and smiled at the birds chirping from the trees lining the short stone wall. Ah, peace and quiet. A godsend. Especially after last night.

She thought she'd been prepared to see Stephen again. After four years, she thought her silly heart had learned its lesson and hardened just enough to be immune to his grins and charms. That having discovered the hard way the dangers of losing one's heart to the wrong man she would know better than to put herself into harm's way again with that smooth-tongued devil.

Apparently not. Because he was all she'd been able to think about during the long sleepless night she spent pacing in her bedroom. How he'd said he'd missed her. How he'd asked her to forgive him. How he wanted to be friends again.

Friends? Ha! She'd seen the look in his eyes when he'd tried to kiss her, and it certainly wasn't friendship that lingered there.

He'd said he'd changed, but had he really? Oh, he'd grown fully into manhood. *That* much was clear with every glance. It was also tantalizingly obvious beneath her hands when they'd rested against the hard muscles of his shoulders. Yet the changes weren't only physical. A sobriety lingered in him that hadn't been there before.

But the same empty flattery and compliments, the same taking of convenient kisses...Had he truly changed from the self-centered young man he'd been, when he'd cared for no one and nothing but his own selfish desires? If she let him back into her heart and he hadn't changed, how would she ever recover if he wounded her again? He'd sliced open her heart the first time. A second might shatter it irreparably.

A howl pierced the quiet, followed by sharp curses

and the sound of a hard object hitting a soft one. Another heartbreaking howl—

Faith ran.

Ahead in the road, a large stranger held a shaggy wolfhound by the scruff of his neck and beat at it with a club. The dog's eyes were wide with fear, its tail tucked between its legs. It struggled to break free as the club struck brutally against its head. A bone-chilling howl of pain tore from its throat.

Faith made a diving grab for the hound just as the man raised his arm to strike again. "Leave that dog alone!"

The man hesitated in his swing when she threw her arms around the dog's neck. Then he let out a violent curse that set the animal into a fit of snarling barks. "That damn cur tried to bite me!"

"That's no reason to beat him!" she defended, sliding as much of her body between the man and the wolfhound as possible. If the brute wanted to hurt an innocent creature, then he'd have to go through her to do it! "He thought you were trying to hurt him."

"I'll sure as hell hurt him now!"

The man grabbed her arm and yanked hard to pull her away from the dog, who instantly began to snarl and snap at the man. He kicked at the hound, and the animal latched onto his leg, sinking its teeth into his calf.

With a curse, he viciously kicked the dog loose. He swung the club again, just barely missing Faith's head. So close she felt the whoosh of air against her cheek.

A gunshot split the air.

The man spun around in surprise, his hand clamped tightly over the club and holding it above his head, ready to strike. He stepped back just far enough for Faith to see—

Stephen.

He sat on his horse in the middle of the lane, with one arm raised into the air and a trail of smoke curling from the end of the spent pistol in his hand. His face remained hard and emotionless, and Faith shivered. She'd never seen him looking so fierce before. So deadly.

"The lady said to leave the dog alone," he said calmly, his deep voice coldly controlled. "So if I were you, I'd release her." He slowly raised a second pistol in his other hand and pointed it at the man's chest. "And step away."

The man shoved her to the ground beside the dog, who immediately darted between her and the stranger to protect her. The hair along its back stood on end as a low, threatening snarl emanated from between its bared teeth.

"Damned bitch!" The man tossed the club down at her feet and then spat at the ground. "As worthless as that mangy cur."

White-hot rage flickered in Stephen's eyes, but he

calmly kept the pistol pointed at the man. "You're a stranger to this area."

"That's none of your goddamned bus—"

"Or you would know that she is Lady Faith Westover, daughter of the Duke of Strathmore."

The man's red face paled to white.

"Who will surely set you swinging by the neck for touching her."

"But I-I didn't—I didn't!" He glanced down at her, and his eyes widened as he finally took in the quality of her clothes and the fairness of her face. "I-I...My apologies, my lady! But that dog bit at me, and I was only—"

"Leave," Stephen ordered in a voice so filled with raw fury that an icy shiver slithered down Faith's spine. He cocked the pistol. "Now."

The man ran down the lane and plunged into the woods. Within seconds, he was gone from sight. By nightfall he'd be two villages away. A ragged sigh of relief poured from her.

Stephen eased down the hammer, then dismounted from his horse. As he tucked both pistols beneath his redingote, he came forward slowly, watching the dog and carefully keeping his distance from its snapping jaws.

"Good boy," she told the hound in the calmest voice she could muster, despite the fierce pounding of her heart.

"Hush now."

At her soft words, the animal stopped barking and with a whimper spun around to race back to her. It buried its furry head against her shoulder, and all of it shook violently with fear. Petting it soothingly, Faith rolled her eyes that her guard dog had turned out to be not so fierce after all. Because for all he'd hated the man who'd struck him, he didn't give a single growl or snarl as Stephen knelt on the ground beside her. *Traitor.*

"Are you all right?" Concern thickened his voice.

"I'm fine." Although her dress was completely ruined, both by the ground where she'd fallen when the man shoved her and now by the ripe smell of dirty dog.

He tugged off his gloves and with a worried frown reached for her chin, to turn her head from side to side as he studied her for any signs of wounding. Heaving out a breath of relief, he wrapped his arms around her and pulled her tightly against him.

"Dear God, Faith," he murmured, his mouth buried in her hair. "What were you thinking, to confront a man like that? You could have been seriously injured."

"I wasn't hurt," she protested. She closed her eyes and drank in the strength of his arms around her, the hardness of his body pressed against hers. She'd missed being in his arms more than she'd realized, more than she should have let her herself feel. Even though she knew she should push him away, she couldn't find the resolve to do so.

"When I saw that bastard raise that club—" A soft curse passed his lips. He cupped her face between his hands as he admitted in a raspy murmur, "If he'd hurt you, I would have killed him."

Her lips parted softly at the intensity in him. She'd never seen him like this before. Never this angry, never this upset. And that it was because of her—

No. She wouldn't let her foolish heart get its hopes up this time, only to be dashed again when he turned his attentions away. Or when he decided to leave again.

"Faith," he whispered and leaned in to kiss her.

She froze, her breath catching in her throat and all of her tensing as his lips moved gently against hers. For one desperate moment she was certain that even her heart had stopped beating. He was kissing her—Stephen was *kissing* her! Oh heavens. She should have shoved him away, should have slapped him, should have done...*anything* except sit there and let him.

But moving away was the last thing she wanted to do. Not when the protective warmth of his arms and the taste of his kisses were so bittersweet that she couldn't find the strength to deny herself of them. And certainly not when his kiss ached, filled with such longing that she trembled from it.

He kissed her as if he needed this embrace to survive, as much as he needed air to breathe. Its intensity stunned her. So did her own heart-thumping response to it, how her blood heated and her flesh tingled. How she thrilled at the way his mouth so easily took possession of hers.

Confusion spun through her, and an aching rose low in her belly. Stephen was kissing her, and it was just as wonderful as she remembered. No...not just as wonderful. *Better.* So much better because when he'd left he'd still been a man-boy, full of fire and urgency. Now he was all man, and the rashness inside him had tempered into control, making him all the more dangerous because of it.

"Faith," he whispered achingly as he tore his mouth away from hers and trailed his lips along her jaw. "Beautiful Faith...how much I missed you..."

She squeezed her eyes shut against the stinging tears. Instead of thrilling her, his words angered her. Her heartache ran too deep to be assuaged by mere words. He'd flattered and flirted with her before, after all, only to break her heart. He'd kissed her hungrily four years ago, too, lavished her with compliments and flattery, and it meant nothing in the end.

"Not enough," she whispered sadly, turning her face away.

"What do you mean?" His lips found her ear and

sucked at her earlobe, and she couldn't fight down the delicious tingles that vibrated through her.

"You left." A confusion of conflicting emotions rioted inside her, half of which had her wanting to shove him away and the rest making her thrill at the way his muscles flexed beneath her fingertips, tempting her to simply throw her arms around him and surrender. "With no warning, no explanation..."

"I couldn't stay." Regret roughened his voice even as his arms tightened around her, as if he could read her mind and sense her doubt. As if he were afraid she might slip away. "I had to leave. England was unbearable for me, you know that. There was too much pressure from my family to be something I wasn't, too many responsibilities for the marquessate, and my father..." He drew a jerking breath at the memories of that time. "Daniel had already enlisted. The regiment was leaving—"

"You left," she repeated, unable now to stop the tears from gathering at her lashes, the sobs from choking in her throat. "You left *me*."

"I was a damned fool, I know that now." He placed a kiss against her lips, so tender that it stole her breath away. "Forgive me, Faith." Another kiss, this one lingering long enough for his hands to sweep tenderly over her body. "Give me a second chance."

Her chest clenched so painfully that she winced. Those were the exact words she'd longed to hear for the past four years, for him to realize what a cad he'd been and how much he'd lost when he left her. But sweet words and empty flattery had always come easily to him. How could she believe him about this?

His lips cajoled at hers to open so he could slip his tongue inside, and when she did, helpless now to push him away, a wanton sensation curled through her, sliding down her spine until her toes curled beneath her. Oh heavens, he'd curled her *toes*! More, a wicked ache began to throb between her legs. Through a fog of desire, her mind couldn't think of the right thing to do at that moment. She knew only the longing that blossomed inside her and the delicious slide of his tongue between her lips in a tantalizing rhythm that had her grasping at his shoulders to keep from falling away with him into oblivion.

He rained kisses along the side of her neck, never kissing the same spot twice before moving on, as if he wanted to explore and taste every bit of her. She couldn't fight back the urge to lean into him, to press herself as tightly against him as she could. When she arched her back and brought her breasts against his lapels, she was rewarded with a soft groan of appreciation.

As if he knew how close she was to capitulation, he

slid his hand up to her neck and massaged slow circles against her nape. Such an innocent touch, yet the possessiveness of his hand on her and the seductive caresses of his fingertips conveyed exactly how much pleasure he could give her if she simply let go. If she forgave him and somehow found a way to erase the past four years of loneliness and tears.

"Faith," he murmured. "I've changed. Let me prove it to you." He took her bottom lip between his and sucked until he pulled the faint ache from between her legs all the way up through her body. "Say you'll give me a second chance."

Her breath came fast and shallow as his hand at her waist began to slide slowly upward over her ribs, higher and higher...When he cupped her breast, holding her fullness against his palm, a hot yearning shot through her with a fierce intensity she'd never felt before. He murmured her name and strummed his thumb over her nipple, and the soft friction made her shiver. She whimpered as every inch of her tingled with a desperate longing to be touched even more intimately.

"I've made terrible mistakes, Faith, but I swear to you that I will do everything in my power to correct them." As his hand continued to caress her breast and tease at her nipple through her dress, the other one traced delicate patterns at her nape, and he placed a soft kiss against her throat, so tenderly that it stole her breath away. "Forgive me, Faith."

"I don't—I can't—" she panted out, not knowing what to say or think. Her mind whirled beneath the heat of his touch, which was somehow both wicked and wonderful. She felt as if she were spinning out of control, and the emotions he churned inside her turned unbearable—

"No!" She shoved away from him, her eyes blurring with anger and tears.

Desperate to get away, she scrambled to her feet and snatched up her bonnet, then hurried down the lane as fast as she could without breaking into a run. Her chest heaved in painful gasps as she struggled to catch back the breath he'd stolen. She blinked rapidly. The devil take the man! What right did he have to come sweeping back into her life like this, to think he could pick up where he left off—kissing her, no less! As if he had the right to take kisses from her whenever he liked, then flatter her into doing his bidding.

Oh, he hadn't changed at all! He was still the same scoundrel he'd always been.

He fell easily into step beside her, his horse clip-clopping along behind and the wolfhound following at her heels. Her stomach plummeted. Oh perfect! She'd created a parade, when all she wanted was to be left alone.

"You have no right to kiss me," she scolded, her eyes

fixed straight ahead. He didn't deserve her attention, not even a glance! Besides, if she did look at him, she'd see those smooth cheekbones of his, that curly dark hair that was perfect for running fingers through, those sensuous lips—*Drat him!* Why on earth did he have to be so blasted attractive? And why, oh *why*, did he have to be a rake who knew how to kiss so well? "Certainly *not* to touch me like that."

"None at all," he agreed ruefully. "My apologies."

That earned him an annoyed dart of her eyes. "Or to ask my forgiveness when you don't deserve it."

"I truly don't."

Another irritated flick of her gaze in his direction. "And do not assume that just because you came riding in like Horatio Nelson on horseback—"

"*Admiral* Nelson?"

"Yes—No!" Why did she lose the ability to think when she was around him? Oh bother! "You know what I mean. Just because you chased that man away doesn't give you any claim to me."

"None whatsoever," he said in the same chagrinned tone as before, but Faith could have sworn she heard a deeper edge to his voice.

"Because you don't." The words tumbled from her as rapidly as her steps. "I believed you once before, you know.

All those things you said, all the compliments you paid me...I believed that you cared about me, only to be hurt. *Deeply* hurt, Stephen."

"That was my mistake," he said softly.

That caught her off-guard, and she stumbled across a bump in the lane. He caught her arm to steady her but didn't release her once she'd moved on.

Her heart somersaulted with a moment's hope—Then the silly thing crashed down into the pit of her stomach because she knew he hadn't changed at all. Feeling like a fool all over again, she yanked her arm away.

"You have no right to kiss me like that," she admonished, "just because you wanted to."

"I did want to," he murmured, this time not at all remorseful. "I truly did."

She ignored the knotting inside her belly. "We are only friends."

"Friends who kissed," he clarified. "With great passion."

"There wasn't any great passion," she grated out the lie between clenched teeth, knowing exactly how passionate his kisses were but refusing to give him the satisfaction of admitting *that*.

"There wasn't? Then maybe we should try it again."

The man was impossible! Her frustration with him—

with herself—with *all* of it!—boiled to the surface. "We are *friends*, nothing more," she asserted, knowing she had to acknowledge the truth behind that statement, no matter how painful. "That's all we will ever be."

He murmured, "I wouldn't say *ever*..."

Her breath hitched at the soft promise behind his words, but she knew he wasn't sincere. Painful experience had taught her well what to expect from him. She'd hardened her heart enough to keep him from ever breaking it again, although each heated glance, each breathtaking kiss, and each caressing touch sliced deeper than she wanted to admit.

But he'd played with her affections once. She refused to let him do it again.

"Dunwich and a Strathmore daughter? It's *expected*." She shook her head with a dismissive laugh and repeated his words from last night, "And you never do the expected."

She darted a glance in his direction and found his eyes narrowed and fixed straight ahead, his shoulders stiff, and his jaw clenched tight. Oh, he was *not* happy that she'd laughed at him!

But it was nothing less than the rascal deserved. What had he expected, for heaven's sake? Did he really expect her to take him seriously? Most likely he thought she'd fling herself into his arms and beg to be kissed, grateful for whatever scrap of attention he paid her.

She couldn't blame him for thinking so. After all, she'd once done exactly that.

But *never* again.

A line of demarcation needed to be drawn. "You're the same man you've always been, eschewing the expected in favor of the unpredicted. For example, kissing me back there," she announced with a nonchalant wave of her hand, as if he hadn't shaken her to her core and left her longing for more. "That was very unexpected."

"Not for me," he drawled. "I've wanted to do that since the moment I walked into the ball last night and saw you."

His words sent heat twining down her spine. "Well, it was for me." In more ways than she was willing to count. "You shouldn't have done that."

Taking her shoulders, he stopped her and turned her to face him. "Why not?" His eyes gleamed, as if he wanted nothing more than to pull her back into his arms. "Didn't you enjoy it?"

So much more than I should have. She shook her head to fight back the rising blush. "It doesn't matter if—"

"Because I certainly did." He drove her to fresh distraction with the breathy purr of his voice. "A great deal."

"That's not the point," she dodged.

"I think it's a very important point." He slid a heated

gaze down at her mouth, and for a moment, she thought he might just kiss her again. To prove his very important point.

"Because you deserve to be kissed, Faith Westover," he murmured, lowering his head until his breath shivered against her lips. So close to touching, yet so frustratingly far away..."You deserve to have a man hold you in his arms, to be touched and caressed. To be assured of how desirable you are, the kind of woman who invades a man's thoughts and haunts his dreams." His eyes darkened as he stared into hers. "To realize exactly how much power you hold over him, and how desperately he wants you."

A longing flared hot inside her. "Oh," she whispered breathlessly.

"Yes." His lips curled into a crooked grin. "*Oh*."

She held her breath, waiting for his mouth to seize hers in another gut-twisting kiss—

He suddenly released her shoulders. Turning away, he walked on down the lane, whistling to himself as he went, with the horse sauntering along behind.

Left standing in the middle of the lane, Faith blinked in utter bewilderment at the sting of not being kissed, even as confusion swirled inside her. Because she didn't *want* to be kissed, certainly not in that scandalous way he'd suggested. In that wanton way that would make her feel beautiful and desired, an object of passion and love. That simply wonderful, thrillingly exciting way—

Oh, the devil take him!

She ran to catch up with him, then sniffed haughtily as she fell into step beside him, as if she wouldn't deign even to give him the time of day except that they were walking in the same direction. As if her heart wasn't slamming against her ribs with each pounding beat.

"You shouldn't tease me like that." But her scolding emerged as a throaty murmur.

"I'm not teasing, Faith. Far from it." It wasn't amusement that shone on his face. It was raw determination. "Every night during the past two years, I lay in bed and thought about you, wondering what I could do to make amends for the way I treated you. What it would feel like to kiss you again, to hold you…to hear you laugh or see one of your smiles. And every thought of you made me realize what a damned fool I was to leave you."

She stopped in mid-step, so suddenly that the dog smacked into her legs. The hound fell back onto his haunches and looked up at her, shaking his head with dazed bewilderment. And she stared at Stephen, the same dazed bewilderment clouding her face.

*****

Stephen watched her curiously, waiting for her reply to that wholly improper confession that had left her momentarily speechless and charmingly flustered.

"I don't believe you," she finally said through her stunned surprise, which he was certain she'd meant to utter with all the frosty haughtiness of an octogenarian governess but which actually emerged as a husky purr. "You didn't write, you didn't say of word of this until now..."

"Because you weren't ready to hear it." He still wasn't certain she was, even now.

She gaped at him silently for a long moment, as if she simply couldn't fathom him. Then with an irritated scowl, she spun on her heel and stomped away, the dog once more loping behind at her heels.

Stephen stared after her. So, he'd rattled her. And quite thoroughly, too, judging from the way she kept her back ramrod straight as she hurried away and refused to look back at him.

Good. Because she'd thoroughly rattled *him.*

He hadn't meant to confess his attraction for her, and he certainly hadn't meant to kiss her like that or touch her like *that*—although he found it difficult to regret holding her in his arms. Sweet Lucifer, how much he'd missed her! But now, there was more to her than just the innocent sweetness he remembered, because he'd tasted her desire for him.

If there had been any lingering doubts inside him that Faith wasn't meant for him, her kisses had destroyed them all.

His long strides easily caught up with her shorter ones, made even more stunted because the mongrel at her heels kept getting under her feet in his determination to remain as close to her as possible. When he darted in front of her, she nearly tripped over him.

Stephen grabbed her arm to steady her, saying nothing when she yanked her arm away and kept right on stomping toward home, which now came into sight around a bend in the lane.

He tugged at his gloves to keep his hands busy so he wouldn't make one last attempt to pull her into his arms again before they walked into view from the house. "You should also know that I've made plans for Mary and Jeremy to resettle by next month. Their stay at Elmhurst is only temporary."

She gave a peeved sniff. "That is none of my concern."

Oh yes, it was. Very much. The obstinate woman just didn't know it yet. "Then the rumors about her will die down and—"

"And the others?"

He blinked, puzzled. "Pardon?"

"All the other rumors that have been circulating

77

about you since your return, the ones which have nothing to do with Mary and her son," she clipped out, nearly as quickly as her strides in her hurry to be away from him. "Will those die down, too?"

His chest tightened. "Those aren't true."

"So I'm to believe that you've given up drinking yourself into foxed fits of debauchery?" Accusation dripped from her voice, although he certainly deserved every bit of her displeasure. "That used to be your favorite pastime."

His lips twisted ruefully. That was a very apt description of the shiftless man she'd once known him to be. "Yes, I've given it up."

"Fraternizing with actresses and singers in smoky backrooms of Covent Garden hells?"

"I haven't been to London since my return." He slid her a suspicious glance. How did *she* know what went on in those rooms?

"And when you do travel there eventually?" she pressed. Now that they'd reached the small meadow behind the Hartsfield stables, her pace quickened, as if she couldn't be away from him soon enough. And the uncertain furrow in her brow that he'd put there seemed to deepen with each step. "Am I to believe that you won't spend all your time wagering at the clubs and gaming tables?"

"Believe it," he answered calmly. "Because I plan on

spending all my time with you, Faith."

She halted and stared at him as if he'd just sprouted a second head. Her green eyes widened, and her pink lips formed a surprised O.

He took a single step closer to her, coming as close as he'd dared with the stables only a few yards away. "I'll ask you again," he said quietly, his voice low. "Will you give me a second chance?"

She swallowed, hard. So hard that the urge to place his lips right there against her throat and feel the soft movement for himself hit him so intensely that he shuddered.

"And the gossip about the other women, Stephen?" she whispered. Her words were barely more than a breath, but their indictment was piercing. "All the wives and widows you're...intimate with?"

"There are no other women." He stared into her eyes, trying to make her understand how much she meant to him. "I'm not the same man who left England, no matter what the gossips say."

Doubt glistened in her eyes. "Am I truly to believe that?"

"Yes." That single word was spoken with all the resolve he could muster, and every bit of his tarnished soul.

A peculiar look darkened her face, one he couldn't quite decipher, as she stared at him silently, as if she couldn't find the words to put voice to the emotions swirling inside her. "Stephen..."

But they were unable to say anything more because a groom hurried from the stable to take his horse, ending all further conversation. As he gave instructions for the gelding's care, she backed away to put several feet between them, the rescued hound still at her heels.

"I have to see to the dog," she explained, her fingers twisting nervously in her bonnet's ribbons. "Thank you for the walk."

She turned before he could stop her and practically ran toward the stables to flee from him.

"Faith?" he called out.

Reluctantly, she stopped, and her shoulders stiffened as she turned to face him.

"I want you to be able to trust me."

Her face melted into an expression of deep sadness. "I don't know if that's possible anymore."

Then she hurried toward the stable door, calling to the dog to follow her. But the animal wouldn't have strayed from her side if someone had waved a boiled chicken before its nose for all that he'd latched so possessively onto her. Stephen couldn't blame him. He wanted nothing more himself than to be by her side, now and for the rest of his life. Although he suspected she would have come after him with a club herself if he suggested such a thing to her now.

He *had* changed, damn it, but she wasn't willing to believe it. And he'd never have a chance with her until he proved it.

But for God's sake, how did a man prove what he *wasn't*?

Muttering a curse beneath his breath, he yanked off his gloves and slapped them against his thigh as he started forward toward the stables after her. He couldn't help himself. He was just as besotted as the dog.

As he reached the stable door, Edward Westover stepped out from the stall where he'd been inspecting a horse. His dark gaze met Stephen's. "Dunwich."

He stopped, his spine straightening. "Strathmore."

The duke turned to glance down the wide aisle at Faith as she gave rapid instructions to one of the stable boys about the dog's care. The shaggy beast sat at her feet and scratched a hind foot behind his ear. When he switched legs, he forgot to put the first one down and fell forward onto his nose. Immediately, she knelt down and pulled the dog into her arms, fussing over him even as he joyfully slobbered wet licks across her face.

Stephen shook his head. *Christ.* He was jealous of a damned dog.

"Where did she find this one?" Strathmore asked. The

two men were far enough away that she couldn't overhear. "In the lane near the river. Rescued it from a man who was beating it."

Her father nodded with a heavy sigh. "She's always bringing home one kind of stray or another. And speaking of strays..." He slid Stephen a sideways glance. "She's happy to have you back in England. We all are."

Stephen didn't believe that for a second, but his lips twisted wryly as he answered, "Thank you, sir."

"The duchess and I have always thought well of you, and we've been honored to be your godparents. You were named after my late brother, you know." He smacked his riding crop against the sole of his boot to dislodge a piece of straw clinging to the heel. "We've cared about you as if you were one of our own."

"Yes, sir." His gaze returned to Faith. "And I'm grateful for—"

"Stay away from my daughter."

Stephen slowly turned his head and found Strathmore's dark eyes boring into him. "I would never do anything to harm Faith," he assured him. And meant every word.

"Good to hear it." Strathmore smiled and slapped him good-naturedly on the back. "Because it would be a shame if I had to shoot you."

He walked away toward Faith, who greeted her father with a kiss to his cheek.

Stephen arched a brow. A *damned* shame, indeed.

Chapter Five

Squinting against the afternoon sun the following day, Faith glanced around to make certain that no one was watching. Then she kicked at her ball to send it an extra few yards toward the metal hoop at the end of the alley.

"Cheating at lawn billiards?" Stephen's deep voice drawled at her shoulder. "For shame."

She rolled her eyes. Didn't the man have anything better to do than to continue to annoy her?

"I never cheat at lawn billiards," she corrected with a haughty sniff.

So it was a good thing they were playing pall mall. And cutthroat, at that, in which rules were few and cheating was practically encouraged. Except for directly hitting opponents' balls with their own mallets, players were free to do whatever necessary to drive their balls the length of the alley and through the metal hoop at the end in the fewest number of strokes.

Mama had scheduled an afternoon of games for the guests, for once refusing to let the men go off hunting or fishing. Now everyone was gathered on the lawn, and while the men competed for prizes in rounds of bowls or archery, the women played at pall mall or battledore and shuttlecock. A tent had been erected near the rose garden, beneath which several tables had been placed where guests could take tea and refreshments at their leisure. Footmen scurried back and forth from the house with fresh trays of biscuits, sugared fruits, and sandwiches, pots of tea, and pitchers of lemonade. Several guests lounged on blankets and pillows spread out across the grass, while other couples surreptitiously slipped away into the private spaces of the walled gardens or one of the surrounding follies, where they couldn't be seen from the house.

Mama and the twins presided over all of it as hostesses, making certain that the guests were enjoying themselves, while Faith was certain Papa was hiding in his study. He'd never had patience for lawn games.

Stephen clucked his tongue like a scolding governess and tapped her ball with his foot, sending it back to where it had originally come to rest.

She narrowed her eyes. "Shouldn't you be over with the men?"

"I find the competition here more interesting." His gaze swept over her, and drat him for sprouting goose flesh on her arms! "And far more beautiful."

"Yes, I suppose you would." She wasn't naïve enough to fall for his charms, not even after the way he'd kissed her yesterday in the lane. So if she'd been thinking nearly constantly about those kisses and the tingles he'd set loose inside her, it was only because he'd taken her by surprise. No other reason. She certainly hadn't fallen for him again.

"Compared to Lord Throckmorton plucking a bow, Lady Rathbourne cuts a far lovelier figure swinging a mallet."

He glanced down the long alley to where the viscountess was making an enthusiastic swing to whack her ball several yards through the air and nearly taking off the head of an unsuspecting footman standing nearby. He arched a brow. "Or attempting to fell Sherwood Forest."

Despite herself, Faith laughed, and his eyes softened on her face. Which sent up a whole new round of tingles. Drat him.

But the viscountess must have sensed their gazes on her, for she smiled flirtatiously at Stephen and daintily carried her mallet down the lawn after her ball, swinging her hips in invitation.

Faith scowled. Clearly, the viscountess had other games in mind for this evening.

She lifted her chin. What did it matter to her what designs the scheming woman had on Stephen? She was welcome to the rascal as far as Faith was concerned.

She swung her mallet, hard, and sent her own ball careening through the air toward the far end of the green. "Excuse me," she said. "I'm playing through."

He stared after the little red ball as it bounced several yards away and mumbled, "Obviously."

She grit her teeth and walked away, to put as much distance as possible between them.

But the infuriating man reached down to scoop up his own ball from the grass and carried it with him as he fell into step beside her.

"Now who's the one cheating?" she muttered. "Knowing you, I'm surprised you didn't find a way for your ball to travel by horseback."

He grinned at her, which only earned him another interested glance from the viscountess. "Don't worry, Faith. Victory is securely yours." He lowered his voice and murmured cryptically, "Besides, there are more important things to win than pall mall."

"Well, it certainly seems that Lady Rathbourne is set on winning *you*," she muttered. "She couldn't take her eyes off you last night at dinner." In fact, the woman had stared at him as if she'd rather have devoured him than her roasted pheasant.

"I have no interest in her."

Yet even as he said so, the viscountess brushed her hand across her neckline and over the swells of her large breasts that were nearly spilling out of her corset, which was drawn up so tight that it was a wonder the woman hadn't fainted for lack of breath.

Grinding her teeth, Faith stood over her ball and did her best to ignore both of them as she set up her shot.

"She isn't my sort."

"Then who is these days?" She pulled back her mallet to swing—

"You."

The mallet struck the grass a foot from the ball. A large divot flew high into the air.

She gaped at him. Ignoring the shocked expression on her face, Stephen gazed down at the trench she'd carved in the lawn.

"Seems your aim's a bit off," he mused.

Her mouth slammed shut, and her hands clenched around the mallet handle. He dropped his ball onto the grass next to hers and took the mallet from her, ostensibly to hit his ball but more than likely to keep her from swinging it at his head.

"But keep practicing," he assured her as he took aim,

88

then expertly sent the ball rolling down the green and straight toward the iron ring at the far end. "After all, practice makes perfect."

Wordlessly, she crossed her arms and glared at him, afraid if she spoke she'd certainly say something she regretted. But there was a world of accusation in the stare she leveled on him, and the rascal deserved every cutting bit of it.

"I have no interest in Lady Rathbourne," he assured her, all the teasing gone from him. "Not at this party." He straightened, and his gaze locked onto hers. "Not ever."

She caught her breath at the subtle promise in his words. Had he truly changed, and changed so much that even women like Viscountess Rathbourne no longer tempted him? His blue eyes shined as he held the mallet out to her as if in a peace offering.

"Then someone should tell Lady Rathbourne," Faith mumbled as she took the mallet from him.

He cast a dismissing glance in the viscountess's direction. "I think she'll get the message soon enough. Besides—" His gaze returned to her. "I'd rather spend time with you."

A happy warmth swelled inside her. Ignoring the nervous butterflies dancing in her belly, she turned away to swing at her ball. "So you keep saying."

"You don't believe me?"

She watched her ball go bouncing down the alley, outpacing his by at least half a dozen yards. "No."

She followed after. Stephen fell into step beside her.

She rolled her eyes. Apparently, he was determined to shadow her all afternoon. What his real reason was, though, she had no idea. But it couldn't have been because he wanted to spend time with her. Not this trouble-maker.

"I've been thinking," she ventured quietly, daring to change topics and knowing she was dangerously close to overstepping. "About Mary Halstead and her son...and all the rumors about you two."

"Oh?" He stiffened, but at least he didn't tell her to mind her own business.

So she nodded and hurried on. "A mistress is certainly nothing new, but the gossips are stirred up because she's residing at Elmhurst Park." She added after a pause, "With you. Which makes the situation seem more scandalous than it really is."

"She's only staying until the end of the month," he assured her.

"Where will she go then?"

"To one of my other properties, one far enough away that the rumors will stop."

She shook her head. He'd forgotten exactly how cruel

people in society could be to each other if he believed that was all it would take to end the rumors. "They won't. The gossips will simply think you've had a spat and sent her away, that you'll accept her back at Elmhurst as soon as you want to...*see* her again."

His lips twitched in amusement at her attempt to keep the conversation wholly proper, even though they were discussing rumors about mistresses. "So what do you suggest?"

He took the mallet from her and lined up to take his swing.

"That you find a wife."

He jerked his head up to stare at her just as the mallet hit his ball. It rolled forward, coming to rest against hers. Then he blinked, staring at her as if she'd just vowed to assassinate the queen.

"I think that's a fine idea," he murmured, oddly breathless.

She blew out an aggravated sigh. Leave it to Stephen to tease about this. "I'm serious. If you only send Mrs. Halstead away, no one will believe you've broken off with her. But if you *also* marry, then everyone will assume it's truly ended because of your wife. You'll be just another peer breaking off with his mistress upon marriage." She looked away, unable to fathom the peculiar look he was giving her.

"Besides, you said you wanted to be respectable. So it's time you were married and produced an heir."

"I think that's a *very* fine idea," he drawled huskily over her shoulder as he came up close behind her. Despite herself—and the topic of Stephen marrying someone else— she shivered at the heat she heard in his voice. "Well, *attempting* to produce an heir, anyway. I've heard that practice makes perfect."

She wheeled around to gape at him. A flush heated her cheeks at the thought of Stephen in bed, wrapped in sheets and practicing— *Oh bother!*

The scoundrel knew exactly the effect his words had on her, and a crooked grin pulled at his lips, as if daring her to flirt back. But she would *never*, and certainly not with him!

"Then I suggest," she bit out as she placed her foot on her ball to hold it still, then pulled back her mallet, "that you *practice* with Lady Rathbourne."

She swung with all her might and struck her ball, sending his flying off the course. It sailed toward the chestnut plantation and fell out of sight among the trees.

With a smug smile at her stroke, she took a second swing at her own ball and sent it bouncing down the alley, to land within ten feet of the iron ring. "Good day."

She slung the mallet over her shoulder and strode away, humming happily to herself and relishing the heat of his irritated gaze on her back as she went.

*****

Damn damn damn!

Stephen bit back a curse as he searched through the trees for his ball. Faith certainly wasn't making this easy on him.

But then, why should she? She was right before, when they were walking in the lane and she'd admitted to how much he'd hurt her when he'd left. He'd broken her trust, and although she was one of the most loyal people he knew, once her trust was broken it was extremely hard to get back.

"There are more important things to win than pall mall," he mumbled the reminder to himself as he pushed a bush aside to search the undergrowth. Like Faith's heart. And when it came to that, victory *would* be his.

He snagged his sleeve on a brambly bush and rolled his eyes. Even if it killed him.

A speck of yellow beneath a fern leaf caught his attention, and he blew out a breath of relief at finding the ball. Now he could return to the game and spend the rest of the afternoon flirting with Faith until she came to accept his attentions or ran out of plantations on Hartsfield Park where she could send his ball. Good thing she hadn't taken up archery.

A rustle of fabric sounded behind him, the soft tread of slippered feet beneath the trees.

He smiled. So the little hellcat had come after him. Although he knew she'd followed him only to gloat at his misfortune, life in the military had taught him to take his victories wherever he could get them. Especially since it meant that they were alone in the trees where no one could see them.

He snatched up the ball and teased, "Did you bring the mallet to finish me off?" He turned around, fully prepared to be attacked by Faith's wit—and froze. "Lady Rathbourne."

"Dunwich." The viscountess smiled flirtatiously as she came toward him through the trees, her bonnet dangling by its strings at her side. "You're a very difficult man to get alone."

Not difficult. *Impossible,* as he'd been completely avoiding her. "It's a large party. Lots of guests." Apparently with one even prowling through the trees after him. "I fell into the rough." He held up his ball. "I want to finish the game, so if you'll excuse me—"

She stepped in front of him, blocking his way. "You've been back in England for three months, yet you haven't been to London."

"I've been busy with my estate." He frowned, wishing she would leave him alone.

Instead, she tugged off her gloves and rested her bared hand on his arm. "I'm certain you have been. Which makes one wonder..."

He stiffened with wariness. The damned woman made him feel like prey. "Wonder what?"

A wicked smile curled slowly at her full, red lips. "How much you need to be distracted from all that work."

She stepped closer, trapping him between her body and the brambly bush. Given her reputation, the bush possessed fewer thorns.

His jaw tightened, and he said icily, "Lady Rathbourne, please step aside."

Ignoring him, she reached up to unfasten the buttons at the front of her dress, giving him what would have been an unobstructed view of the top half of her breasts if he'd bothered looking. Which he didn't, keeping his eyes firmly on her face. Although he'd never thought it possible, he had no interest in her bosom.

"What other games might you like to play, hmm?" She pressed herself against him and wrapped her arms around his neck.

He grabbed her arms to put her away from him and

said in a low growl, "You are mistaken."

She gave a throaty laugh at that and slid her hand down his arm to his wrist. "One of the finest rakes in England returns after four years in India, where there were no sophisticated English ladies to satisfy you..." She lifted his hand and brought it to her breast. "Surely, my lord, you're in the mood for all kinds of play."

"Not with you." He tried to pull his hand away, but her hold only tightened, earning him another laugh as she pressed herself into his palm.

"I assure you that I can be quite entertaining." She trailed her lips across his throat as she murmured, "And very pleasing."

His jaw clenched so hard now that the muscles in his neck twitched. A few more seconds of this, and he'd break his vow of never manhandling a woman. "Lady Rathbourne, if you do not—"

"Have you found it yet?" Faith's laughing voice carried down to him as she stepped around one of the trees. "It was no less than what you deserved for—"

She saw them and froze. Her face paled as her eyes darted to his hand, still pressed against the viscountess's breast, her bodice half undone and all of her twined around him. Then she turned and ran.

"Faith, wait!" With a curse, he shoved the viscountess

away and charged after her.

He caught her at the edge of the lawn, just as she broke free of the cover of the trees. She slowed to a walk to keep from drawing attention to herself but didn't stop as she headed straight toward the house, her face red with anger.

"Please let me explain," he said in a low voice, his heart tearing when he saw the smile she forced onto her face for the other guests.

"No," she spat out.

"It isn't what you think—

"What I *think* is that I saw that woman in your arms, with her dress undone and your hand on her...Oh, it doesn't matter! Just leave me alone!"

The irony was biting. The woman he didn't want threw herself at him, while the one he wanted couldn't get away fast enough. *Christ.*

He took her arm and gently stopped her, but she refused to look at him. "I am telling you the truth. Lady Rathbourne came after me into the trees—completely uninvited—and threw herself at me. I was sending her away when you found us."

She said nothing, her gaze fixed on the house.

"I would *never* do anything with that woman, Faith," he said softly, daring to take a step closer even though she stiffened.

"Let go of me," she demanded in a whisper.

The anguish he saw in her broke his heart. He spoke in a low plea, "You have to believe me."

She trembled, shifting away from him with agitation. "I-I can't—I can't be this close to you right now."

Self-recrimination rose inside him, and he bit out tightly, "Because you still won't forgive me for leaving you?"

When she finally looked at him over her shoulder, tears glistened in her eyes.

"Because you *smell* of her," she whispered in a breathless accusation. "Her perfume is all over you."

She gently pulled her arm free. As she walked away, he saw her swipe at her eyes. The small movement sliced through him like a knife.

Chapter Six

"Here you go."

Faith placed the leftover slices of ham from her dinner into a bowl, then set it onto the floor of the stall where she was temporarily housing the wolfhound. Papa had agreed to let her keep him only until she could find him new home. She smiled victoriously at that. He'd said the same thing about the three ducks, five cats, two geese, and a tortoise she'd also brought home in the past year, and all of them still lived at the old dairy barn. He'd come around to accepting this one in time, too.

The dog rushed forward.

"Slow down," she warned.

The dog didn't listen, and within seconds, the meat slices were gone. Faith sighed. If he wasn't sick before, he might very well be after this dinner.

"That was honey-glazed ham with pieces of pineapple

that Mama sent for all the way from the South Pacific, I'll have you know." She scratched behind his ear, but the dog was more interested in sniffing at the plate she'd used to carry out the ham. He rose up on his hind legs, begging to lick it. She sighed in defeat. "Oh, all right. But don't tell anyone I let you do this. Cook will never forgive me."

She set the plate down. As the dog happily licked it clean, his tail swinging so hard from side to side that all of him pivoted in a half-circle around his front legs, she sank onto the hay beside him and stroked her hand over his back.

"We really must come up with a name for you. How about Sam or Charlie?" The dog ignored her. "George?" Thinking even less of that name, he wiped his mouth against her arm, leaving a streak of ham juice on her coat sleeve. "Maybe we should name you Hartsfield."

"I don't think Strathmore would find that amusing," came a deep voice from behind her.

Faith narrowed her eyes but refused to glance at Stephen as he stood at the stall's half-door. "Well, then, *Stephen* it is." She arched a brow and pointed at the dog. "Sit, Stephen, sit!"

The dog stared at her as if she'd gone mad.

And the mongrel at the stall door had the gall to laugh.

She glared over her shoulder at him. "He doesn't

listen any better than you do."

"That's because we strays are all alike." Risking her temper, he opened the door and stepped inside. "I knew I'd find you here. Couldn't resist visiting that dog before you went to bed, could you?"

She was caught. With a peeved sniff, she explained, "I came out here to check on the colt and thought I'd look in on him, too."

Stephen glanced at the empty plate and arched a disbelieving brow. "Just look in, hmm?"

Blast him. With growing aggravation, she bit out, "I wanted to make certain he wasn't upset at being in a strange place. I knew he would have trouble settling down for the night."

At that, the dog let out a wide yawn, circled twice, then dropped to the straw. He let out a loud snore.

"Seems to be settling down just fine," Stephen drawled.

Faith rolled her eyes. Even the hound was against her. But at least *this* animal she could manage. "Shouldn't you be inside," she asked brusquely, "smoking cigars and drinking port with the rest of the men?"

"And pass up the chance to be alone with you in the hay?"

She froze, her hand pausing in mid-pet. His comment

was nothing more than meaningless flirtation; her brain knew that, yet her foolish heart skipped just the same.

Not rising to the bait, she narrowed her eyes and asked directly without any amusement, "Why are you here?"

"I need your help." He knelt beside her and set the small basket he was carrying next to her in the straw.

"With what?" she asked suspiciously. She trusted him as far as she could throw him, and looking at him now, all muscle and broad shoulders, that certainly wouldn't be far.

His blue gaze rose to find hers. "I'm upset at being in a strange place and am having trouble settling down."

She rolled her eyes. Leave it to Stephen to use her words against her. Just to prick at him, she held out the plate and asked with a saccharine smile, "Would you like to lick it, too?"

He said quietly, "I meant in England."

Faith caught her breath. She should have rolled her eyes again, shoved him away, laughed—but something about the sober way he said that gnawed at her. "You don't like being home?" she asked softly, with more concern than he deserved.

He forced a lopsided grin. "Home was four years ago."

Her heart tugged for him. Of course, if she pressed, he would have said he was merely teasing, which was always his way. But she knew better. "You'll have no trouble fitting back into society, if that's what worries you. If your dancing skills are any indication, you've not lost any of your social graces."

He nodded with mock gravity. "Thank God a man's character is measured by quadrilles."

"Three-quarter time, actually," she corrected, a smile of amusement teasing at her lips. "It was a waltz."

"Even better."

The easiness of their banter warmed through her. They were almost as they'd been before, able to tease and flirt without hesitation. *Almost.* Because an undercurrent of tension stood between them so palpable she could feel it. Would they ever be as comfortable around each other as they'd once been?

She grimaced. He'd certainly seemed comfortable enough when he'd been kissing her.

"You've managed to fall right back into the thick of things." She hoped he couldn't hear the suspicion in her voice and mistake it for jealousy. Because she wasn't jealous. Not at all. "Viscountess Rathbourne is a beautiful woman."

She cringed inwardly at herself. Well...perhaps a *little* jealous.

He reached out to pet the dog. "I don't like drool."

"Don't attack a defenseless animal," she countered, peeved that he would do so.

He arched a brow, his eyes sparkling mischievously. "I meant Lady Rathbourne."

A bubble of laughter spilled from her. Her hand flew to her lips in embarrassment, but she couldn't stop. Nor could she ignore the devilish expression on his face. "Perhaps not so defenseless after all."

"Claws that a lioness would envy," he told her, a bit too knowingly for her comfort. "So it's a good thing I have no interest in the viscountess. And that absolutely *nothing* happened between us in the trees, except that she made it known that she was available and I refused."

"It certainly didn't look that way to me," she whispered, her throat tightening.

"Because you arrived at the exact wrong moment." He avoided her eyes as he reached for the basket, and she was glad for it, not wanting him to see the embarrassment and doubt she undoubtedly wore on her face. "You know the man I used to be. Do you really think I'd be careless enough to let myself be caught with a woman in the trees?"

No, he wouldn't. That was a very valid point.

She bit her bottom lip. She *wanted* to believe him, and yet, seeing him with the viscountess upset her more than she wanted to admit to herself. She shook her head. "It doesn't matter to me how you spend your time." *Or with whom.*

He said nothing for a moment, and she suspected that he might call her out for that bald-faced lie.

But he focused his attention on the basket instead. "I thought we should have a midnight picnic." He pulled out two small plates covered with towels and set them aside, then handed her two teacups to hold. "I hope you still like hot chocolate."

He lifted up a ceramic chocolate pot, and her chest warmed at his thoughtfulness. "How could you have possibly remembered that?" she murmured, truly surprised. And impressed.

"I remember everything about you, Faith," he assured her as he lifted the towel from the first plate, and this time she warmed for a whole new reason. "Including that you love croissants." Then the second. "And strawberries."

Her belly tightened with wariness. She didn't let herself believe him. Because if he'd truly remembered such small details about her, then—

No. She wasn't that special to him.

"Everyone likes strawberries," she countered with a dismissive shrug of her shoulder.

"Perhaps." He poured the chocolate into the two cups, then set the pot aside and reached for one of the plump strawberries. "But does everyone like to dunk their strawberries into their chocolate like you do?" He dipped it into the dark liquid, then raised it to her lips. "Open."

Too stunned not to obey, she parted her lips, and he placed the ripe berry into her mouth. The sweet combination of chocolate and strawberry melted deliciously on her tongue, and she ate it slowly, relishing its luxurious taste.

"See?" He dipped a second berry. "I'm not so bad."

"Oh yes, you are. You're a rake who—" He slipped the berry between her lips and cut off the scathing description of his romantic antics that she'd been poised to deliver. But this time when she ate the berry, his dark gaze fell to her mouth, and an unbearable longing to be kissed swirled through her.

He caressed his thumb across her lip and brushed away a small droplet of chocolate. "I'm a rake who...what?" His eyes not leaving hers, he sucked the droplet from his thumb and murmured, "Delicious."

Oh my.

She shoved one of the cups at him, suddenly feeling the need to free her hands, although she couldn't have said whether to reach for him or shove him away. Her mind screamed at her that he was nothing but trouble and still the same scoundrel he'd always been, and wasn't this midnight picnic proving exactly that? But her heart, oh her foolish heart! That traitorous thing wanted nothing more than to let him feed her strawberries all night.

"You're a rake who's fallen right back into his old

ways," she scolded, but it was terribly hard to sound disapproving with those beckoning blue eyes staring at her mouth like that. As if he wanted to devour her the way she'd devoured the berries.

"No, I haven't. If I'd fallen into old habits, I wouldn't be here with you." He took the proffered cup and set it aside, and she realized her mistake as soon as he did—one less barrier between them. "I'd be in the house letting Lady Rathbourne dig her claws into me."

"So why aren't you?" she whispered, half-afraid to hear the answer.

He answered quietly, "I don't want that life anymore."

"I don't believe you." She knew him too well. He'd once epitomized that life.

"And yet, here I am."

She frowned at that, not knowing what to think. He *was* here when he could have been in the viscountess's bed, although she didn't believe for one moment that his motives were pure. "And why is that, exactly?"

He stared into her eyes with a beckoning look that left her trembling. "Because I'd much rather be with you."

"I don't believe *that,* either," she scoffed.

His lips twitched, yet he wisely ignored her comment. Instead, he swiftly changed topics by saying, "What no one ever tells you about life in the army is how exceedingly boring it can be, enough to make a soldier crave battle."

"*Crave* battle?" she repeated, surprised.

He quirked a brow at her as he reached for another strawberry. "Nothing combats *ennui* as effectively as the fear of imminent death."

She laughed, despite herself. Leave it to Stephen to make her laugh over something like that!

"So I spent most of those long stretches of boredom thinking about my life, what I wanted from it, what was important to me." With a thoughtful wrinkle crinkling his brow, he dipped the strawberry into the chocolate. "And I kept coming back to the same answer."

She leaned forward slightly, ready to accept the next berry. "Which was?"

"You."

Her mouth fell open in surprise, and he placed the berry on her tongue. As she choked the berry down, she stared at him, stunned. He couldn't mean...*Impossible.* Yet his handsome face was serious, all his teasing gone.

This time when he caressed his thumb across her bottom lip, he lowered his head to follow after it with his lips.

With a soft sigh, Faith closed her eyes against the touch of his mouth to hers, unable to find enough will power to pull away. This was nothing like the kisses he'd given her in the lane. Those had been full of hunger and need, as if he had to kiss her in order to stay alive. But this kiss...oh, *this* one was soft, gentle, and so very tender. There was no hurry this time, no desperation behind the way his fingertips caressed over her cheek, somehow both soothing and exciting at the same time.

As he brushed his lips back and forth across hers, the flavors of chocolate and berry and man blended together into the most delicious taste she'd ever experienced.

"Faith," he murmured against her lips, "darling Faith...It took Daniel's death to make me realize all that I'd been missing, that I'd made a terrible mistake in leaving you."

Her chest tightened with a pang of pain and regret. "Stephen..." she protested in a whisper.

He lifted his head to stare down at her. His blue eyes turned smoky in the shadows cast by the lantern as they searched her face for answers she couldn't give. All she knew was that his return had sent her head spinning and her heart aching. Stephen had always been special to her, and even though she'd been courted by other men since he'd left, they had been nothing but dim shadows compared to his light. If that last summer had gone differently, if he had ever once attempted to bare his feelings like this—

But he hadn't. And nothing could be gained now by wishing for might-have-beens.

Yet when his lips covered hers again, she drank him in, helpless to keep herself from finally accepting the kisses she'd yearned for so long to have. She knew he didn't care for her, knew he'd only end up hurting her again if she once more gave over her heart...but at this moment, here, he was hers. And she wasn't strong enough to deny herself this moment in his arms.

He cupped her face in his hands so that he could more easily take small kisses and nibbles at her lips. "I want to correct all the mistakes I've made, to make right everything that went wrong."

"I don't know—" A caressing sweep of his tongue between her lips silenced her. She shivered at the exquisite intimacy of his kiss as he explored the recesses of her mouth, then set to slowly plunging between her lips in a steady rhythm that had her heart pounding in time to the gentle thrusts of his tongue.

He slid his mouth away from hers to kiss along her jaw and back to her ear. "Before India, I thought I could keep living my life exactly as I had." His lips caressed warmly against her temple. "But I was wrong."

With each soft confession and caress, the heartbreak he'd caused her receded a little more, until there was only Stephen in the shadows. Until all that mattered was the sound of his deep voice falling through her like warm summer rain and the tender caresses of his hands making her feel desired. Instead of pushing him away as she should have done, she clung to him. She knew she was dancing a razor's edge, attempting to savor his kisses while somehow still protecting her heart, but she couldn't help herself. As always, he was irresistible.

"The man I was at the time reveled in doing the exact opposite of what my family and society wanted," he admitted, lowering his head until his mouth was so close that she felt the heat of his lips shivering across hers. "But that's changed now, too."

"Has it?" she whispered breathlessly.

He nodded, the slight movement brushing his lips above hers in a ghost caress that didn't quite touch. "I've decided to marry one of Strathmore's daughters after all."

She stared at him, wide-eyed, not daring to believe the implication behind his words. "What do you—" Something hot and wet licked beneath her chin. She gasped. "Stop that!"

He froze, but the lick came again.

"Oh!" She pulled back, and the wolfhound jumped between them to lap eagerly at her face, slobbering over her cheeks. She tried to push him away, but the dog thought she wanted to play and dove in for another round of licks. Its tail wagged so hard that its entire back half sashayed from side to side.

"That's enough out of you." Stephen grabbed the dog by its collar and pulled it away.

Faith scrambled to her feet. Scowling with a disgusted face, she dragged the back of her hand across her mouth to wipe away the slobber. *Ugh!* She wanted a hot bath.

With a crooked grin, Stephen scolded the dog as he opened the stall door and let him out into the aisle, "Go find your own woman." His midnight blue eyes heated as they lingered on her. "This one's mine."

Her heart lodged painfully in her throat. "I'm not yours, Stephen," she protested softly. "I've never truly been yours."

His grin sobered, and he asked quietly, "Do you want to be?"

Stunned, she searched his face, her heart pounding in utter bewilderment. After all that had happened between them, all the pain he'd caused her, he couldn't seriously be offering...*His.* There was a time when she'd have given everything to be just that, the one woman he loved and cherished, the only woman he wanted in his bed and at his side for the rest of his life. But instead of giving his love, he'd broken her heart. It took four long and lonely years to put it back together, piece by painful piece.

Now he stood here in front of her, the taste of him

still on her lips, and hinted that she could have him if she simply asked. It was everything she'd always wanted from him. And yet...

The truth shivered coldly through her for why he'd been so relentlessly pursuing her, and her heart broke anew. He still didn't want *her*. What he wanted was society's acceptance, and he was willing to go so far in his desire to have that new-found respectability that he would resort to doing that which he loathed most—*the expected*.

And nothing was more expected than marrying Strathmore's daughter.

The roar of blood in her ears was deafening, and each pounding beat jarred her back to reality. To the man Stephen truly was rather than the man she wanted him to be.

She shook her head, his handsome face blurring from the tears stinging her eyes. "It doesn't matter what I want," she breathed, barely above a whisper. "Because you don't want me."

His gaze never left hers as he closed the distance between them, then scooped her into his arms. As he lowered her to the straw, his mouth claimed hers in a blisteringly possessive kiss that left her weak and trembling beneath him.

He tore his mouth away from hers to nip at her throat.

He panted out against her racing pulse, "I very much want you."

Her heart somersaulted. Oh, foolish thing! She *knew* better...An agonized whisper tore from her, "No, you don't."

He lifted his head to stare down at her, and his eyes gleamed devilishly. "I think I do."

She shook her head as the truth choked from her—"You've never wanted *me*, Stephen. Not before, and not now."

His eyes flared as his gaze bore down into hers, and an intensity burned inside him that made her shiver. "Is that what you think?"

"I know so." Four years ago he'd wanted the innocent kisses and flattering attentions of a girl who thought he was dashing beyond compare. Now he wanted respectability at all costs. But he didn't want *her*.

He laughed, the sound dark as it rumbled into her. "You don't know a thing."

*****

Faith gazed at him with such a bewildered expression that Stephen had to bite back a curse. For God's sake, how could she *not* know how he'd felt about her?

His feelings for her went beyond the friendship they'd shared to become something deeper, more enduring, and incredibly special. Her kindness and gentleness toward everyone, the selfless way she had of helping those in need, her wit and cleverness...the heart of an angel encased in a bewitching body. When that terrible battle in India was over, all he could think about was her. All he wanted was to hold her in his arms.

He'd lost her once. He'd be damned before he let her slip away again.

He moved away from her to sit back against the wall, resting his forearm over his bent knee and keeping plenty of distance between them. She smelled too good of lavender, felt too soft and warm— If he'd stayed next to her like that, he'd seduce her right here in the hay and prove himself to be the rake she'd accused him of being.

"The summer when I returned from university and saw the woman you'd become, I wasn't prepared for that," he explained as she sat up and drew her legs beneath her, pieces of straw clinging to her deliciously rumpled hair and that man's coat which would have looked absurd on any other woman. On Faith, it only magnified her unconventional personality. Just one more trait he adored about her. "You'd always been nothing more to me than a friend, and I thought that was exactly where I could keep you." He blew out a deep breath. "I was wrong. That first kiss changed everything."

Even from three feet away, he could feel her catch her breath, so alert was he to every move she made.

"All my life I ran from responsibility. I was expected to behave like a peer from the time I was a child, so I did everything I could to prove I wasn't respectable. Getting expelled from school, drinking and gambling—"

"Whoring," she interjected, none too kindly.

"That, too." He grimaced. "So of course I had no plans for a respectable life. Which was why I joined the army, because it was the last thing anyone expected." His gaze softened on her. "And I certainly didn't expect you, Faith."

"Me?" The word was a throaty purr that swept through him like a warm breeze.

"You'd turned into a woman without anyone noticing. Beautiful and beguiling...and I had no idea what to do with you." She looked away in embarrassment, and he resisted the urge to reach for her. "Well, that's not entirely true. I knew exactly what I *wanted* to do with you, and none of it was respectable."

Her surprised gaze darted back to him, and embarrassment flushed her cheeks.

Pleasure spread through him at her reaction. She wouldn't blush like that if she didn't have feelings for him, no matter how much she denied them.

"Do you know how hard it was to kiss you, Faith, then

walk away? Do you have any idea how great a temptation you were?" He shook his head, remembering those confused and dark days, when the only bright light in his life was Faith. "But marriage to anyone back then, even to you, would have felt like a trap. So I kept my distance."

Her lips parted delicately in surprise. For once, he'd stunned her speechless.

"Until now." He pushed himself away from the wall and crawled toward her, until he was once again poised over her. "Now I've returned a better man, all because of you, Faith."

Then he lowered his head and kissed her thoroughly, tasting the strawberry and chocolate that still lingered there. More—he could taste her desire for him, and he thrilled with it.

He cupped her face against his palm to hold her mouth steady beneath his as he plundered the kiss and thrust his tongue between her lips in a heated promise of what pleasures he could give her if she let him. And not only physical ones. He would give her a home and family, keep her safe, and do whatever he could to make her happy and their lives filled with laughter.

"I want you, my darling," he whispered as he slowly lowered himself until his body covered hers, not slowing in the kisses he scattered across her cheeks, eyes, and lips. "*All* of you, from now until I take my last breath."

This was what had filled his dreams during those long, lonely years in India...the possibility of holding Faith in his arms, tasting the sweetness of her lips, letting the joy of being with her cascade through him. But those dreams paled in comparison to the reality of her, and he was more certain about his love for her than he'd ever been about anything else in his life.

"Marry me, Faith," he whispered against her lips, longing for her to kiss her reply to him.

But when her answer came, the single word tore through him like a slashing blade— "No."

She pushed herself out from under him and scrambled to her feet. As she stepped away, he pursued and closed the distance between them until her back hit against the wall. Then he took another step, trapping her in place.

He lowered his head until their faces were even, his eyes locked onto hers. "Why not?" he demanded, fighting down his frustration and the fresh fear of losing her again. Even now, he trembled with it.

"You know why," she whispered, blinking hard at the tears glistening in her eyes.

His gut knotted guiltily at the sight. *Damnation.* The last thing he wanted to do was hurt her.

"I truly don't," he assured her softly. He reached to

stroke his knuckles across her cheek, but she turned her face away. "Is it Mary Halstead? Getting married will end all the rumors, you said so yourself. We'll face down the gossips together." He stiffened as a terrible new thought struck. "Or is this about the viscountess? I told you—nothing happened."

"No." A ragged shudder passed through her. "It has nothing to do with them."

Relief surged through him at her declaration, and he leaned toward her until their two bodies nearly touched. "Then why not, Faith?"

Squeezing her eyes shut, she shook her head, refusing to answer.

"I know you like me," he drawled. "We've always gotten along well." He shifted forward, finally bringing himself against her. Her breath caught at the contact. "And I can feel how much you enjoy my kisses, so it can't be that."

He captured her mouth beneath his. Despite her protests that she didn't want to marry him, she leaned into him and met the hunger in his kiss, returning the embrace with a need that matched his own. Whatever her reason for refusing him, it wasn't a lack of desire, and his chest swelled with a mix of relief, hope, and love. More love for her than he ever thought possible.

Unable to resist touching her, he trailed his hand down the side of her body and over the curves that even the draping coat couldn't hide. She moaned softly as his hand cupped her breast and began to caress her through the coat and all the other layers beneath, layers he desperately wanted to strip away. How she could feel anything through all that he had no idea, nor did he care when she gave over to her pleasure and arched her back to press herself harder against his hand.

He tore his mouth away from hers to let her catch her panting breath, and he smiled affectionately against her temple as she fisted his lapels to keep him close. "Like that, too, do you?"

"Maybe," she admitted grudgingly, and he bit back a laugh at her. "Well, *I* definitely like it." When he lowered his mouth to her ear and traced his tongue along the outer curl, she whimpered. He groaned out, "A great deal."

He trailed kisses down the side of her neck until his mouth hit the coat collar that was buttoned to the top. He bit back a curse. The only thing that kept him from stripping off that coat and continuing to kiss his way down her body was knowing that she'd soon be his wife. He could be patient until then. *Maybe.*

"You can't deny it," he rasped out as his lips returned to hers. "You can't deny that you have feelings for me, that you don't want a life together as much as I do." He licked teasingly across her lips. "Or that you want me just as much as I want you."

"Want...isn't love," she challenged in breathless pants as his hand fumbled at the buttons keeping the coat closed and her body away from him. "And you...don't love me."

But he did. He'd loved her for years, since long before he left for India, despite being too young and stupid to act on it. But admitting that now would only frighten her. Hell, it frightened *him* when he thought about the enormity of it. "I wouldn't say that," he replied carefully, slipping one button free and then the next until the coat gaped open. His fingers slipped inside—

"But you love the idea of respectability more."

Her whispered words snarled around his heart, and his hand stilled just as it found her low-cut bodice. Surely, he'd misheard..."Pardon?"

"You were once a scapegrace who cared for no one and nothing but yourself," she whispered, the pain of each word reflected on her face. "I'm not naïve enough to think that you couldn't fall back into your old ways."

"I won't." *Good God.* Is that what she truly thought of him? That he was still as unpredictable as that, even after all he'd revealed to her?

Her eyes glistened with tears. "And the women?"

"What women?" Dread surged through him. "There are no other women in my life." There was only Faith. There would only *ever* be her.

"When someone like Lady Rathbourne tempts you—"

"I am *not* tempted by that woman." *Damnation, I love you!* But he definitely couldn't say that now. She wouldn't believe him. "I don't want her, nor anyone like her." He captured her face between his hands, willing with every beat of his heart for her to believe him. "And I will never leave you, Faith. I learned my lesson before."

Sadness darkened her face as she breathed out, "So did I."

He flinched as her whisper pierced him. "I'm not that man anymore. I need you to believe that."

She squeezed her eyes shut to fight back the tears and whispered, "I don't know what to believe."

"Believe that I care about you and would never hurt you." He touched his lips to hers and felt her inhale a sharp breath. "Believe that I need you and *only* you." Another kiss, and this time, he could taste the anguish on her lips. "That I want to be a respectable man for *you*, Faith." He rested his forehead against hers and fought down the nervous beating of his heart. He repeated, "Marry me."

"No, Stephen," she choked out. "I won't."

"Oh yes." A deep voice echoed through the stall and startled them both. "You certainly will."

Wheeling away from her, Stephen glanced up. His

heart stopped. "Strathmore."

Edward Westover stood at the stall's entrance, a murderous look flashing across his face. Stephen was certain that only the duchess's presence at his side—and her hand on his arm—stopped the man from killing him right there in the stable rather than calling him out for pistols at dawn.

Faith placed her hand protectively in Stephen's. "Papa, this isn't what you—"

"Both of you in my study," Strathmore ordered. "*Now.*"

Chapter Seven

Faith stood in her father's study and stared at the rug. She didn't look up. She didn't have to. She knew exactly what expression would be on everyone's face...the anger on Papa's as he sat behind his desk, the patient concern on Mama's as she stood close to his side, and on Stephen's—the scoundrel!—would be smug satisfaction that he'd gotten exactly what he wanted.

While on *her* face everyone could surely read the humiliation over being caught with him, as well as the guilt churning inside her stomach that she'd enjoyed being in his arms. Far more than she should have. While rakes could be reformed and eventually brought into society's good graces, she wasn't certain that Stephen could be.

For all of his cajoling to marry him and the promises of his sweet kisses, how could she be certain that he'd really changed? If he broke her heart a second time, how would she survive?

"So you went to check on the dog," Papa said more calmly than Faith would have given him credit for.

She nodded. There was no point in trying to squirm her way out of this mess. Or avoid the storm to come.

He turned to Stephen. "And you met her there?"

"Yes, sir, I did."

"Why?" That single word held a world of accusation, and Faith winced.

Without a bone of trepidation in his body, Stephen answered, "So I could ask Lady Faith to marry me."

She bit back a frustrated groan. Didn't the rascal realize that he was only making things worse?

But of course he did. One glance at him proved it. He stood perfectly straight, wearing that same military bearing as her father. He didn't even have the decency to cower in front of Papa, as any other man would have done at being caught kissing his daughter.

"A gentleman asks a lady's father when he wants to wed her," Papa admonished angrily.

Standing silently at his side, her mother placed her hand on his shoulder. Most likely Mama was there only to keep Papa from frightening the other party guests by killing Stephen on the front lawn.

Papa's gaze never left him. "The general raised you

well enough to respect that."

"Yes, sir."

Faith saw the curl of Stephen's lips and caught her breath with dread, knowing what was coming—

"But my *mother* raised me to respect the wishes of the lady to whom I propose."

Mama's lips twitched, and she turned her face away before Papa could see the smile threatening there. Her mother had always been a wise woman when it came to dealing with her father.

But Stephen's charms didn't work on Papa, who narrowed his eyes to slits and demanded in a tone so low, so intense that it sent a chill slithering down Faith's spine, "And exactly how is pawing my daughter in a horse stall being respectful?"

Oh God. Her shoulders sagged with mortification. If she hadn't been so humiliated, she would have found the ordeal her father was putting Stephen through amusing. And nothing short of what the scoundrel deserved.

"It wasn't," Stephen admitted ruefully, and Faith nearly rolled her eyes, certain he didn't feel an ounce of remorse. "But in my defense, I had just asked Lady Faith to marry me, and she was in the middle of accepting."

She gaped at him. Oh, that devil! She most certainly was *not*—

"Faith," Papa said, incredibly calm and even more threatening because of it, his gaze sliding across the room to her, "do you agree with Dunwich's version of events?"

"No," Faith answered softly.

"No?" Papa rose to his feet, every inch of him the imposing duke who left men across England shaking in their boots. Faith suspected that the only thing standing between Stephen and a good pulping by Papa would be her careful answer to his question.

She drew a deep breath, needing more courage than she'd ever needed in her life. "I was not accepting his proposal," she corrected softly, raising her eyes to meet her father's. "I will not marry him."

It was Papa's turn then to inhale deeply, and she suspected that breath kept him from exploding. That, and her mother's hand which suddenly returned to his shoulder. "You are a duke's daughter, and you were found alone at midnight in the arms of a man."

A snake, more like it. Stephen had so carefully packed for the picnic. Had he planned on being discovered, too? After all, he'd admitted to her tonight that too much of a rake lingered inside him to be caught with a woman.

"I know," she admitted, "and I regret it." Although, if she were honest, what she regretted was getting caught, not kissing him. Yet she couldn't bring herself to look at Stephen, even though she felt the weight of his gaze on her. "But it was only a kiss, and no one else saw. No one else need ever find out."

Then she did sneak a glance at him, only to see his jaw clenched so tightly that the muscles in his neck jumped. Apparently, he hadn't thought of that loophole in his plan.

"I'm a peer and a soldier," he countered. "I take responsibility for my actions."

That answer had Papa's eyes gleaming with respect. Drat him!

"I will not marry you," she repeated. She looked pleadingly at her mother. "You always said that you wanted your children to find love matches, one as wonderful as what you share with Papa. Stephen and I..." *Do not love each other.* But she couldn't bear to utter that aloud. Her eyes stung with unshed tears as they moved to her father, whose solemn gaze nearly undid her. "It was a kiss, Papa, that was all." Her words were barely above a quiet whisper. "Would you truly force me to marry because of a kiss?"

When her father's gaze met hers, she caught her breath. What she saw pass over his face wasn't anger at being defied but deep disappointment, and the look sliced into her heart. It was a wound she knew might never heal, for both of them.

"Faith," her mother said delicately, her face filled

with concern, "if anyone learns of what is between you two—"

"Nothing is between us." There *was* nothing except friendship, and even that she wasn't so sure of any longer. Because he certainly hadn't stirred feelings of friendship inside her when he'd kissed her. She lifted her chin resolutely and charged ahead, "I will *not* marry a man who wants to wed me only because it's expected."

Stephen's gaze darted to her, the depths of his eyes afire. "That is *not* why I want to marry you."

"Isn't it?" she challenged softly. "You returned to England set on starting a new life, on showing everyone that you've changed. On being respectable."

"Yes, I did." Firm resolve satiated his answer.

"So you'll do whatever it takes to prove that." Her heart pounded so hard that each beat reverberated like the strike of a hammer on iron. "Including doing exactly what's been expected of you all along, no matter how much it grates."

"Is that what you think, that the idea of marrying you *grates* me?" A smile of relief pulled at his lips. "I can assure you that you are not—"

"And when you've grow tired of the expected, when you feel—" She choked on the word, the same word he'd used to describe what he once thought of marriage to her,

"Trapped?"

His smile instantly vanished. "I won't. I've explained to you—" He cut himself off, as if suddenly remembering that the duke and duchess were in the room. "You still think the worst of me." He shook his head in disbelief. "What can I say to convince you, Faith?"

As she looked at him, her heart broke, because she knew the truth. That she had ached too fiercely for too long for him. That she'd spent too many nights crying over him and too many hours wondering what was wrong with her that he didn't stay. She wanted to believe that he'd changed with all her heart and soul, but what proof did she have? She had only his word, and in the past, his word had proved to be nothing but empty flattery.

Misery gripped her as she whispered, "You can't."

He took a step toward her before stopping himself, his hands clenching at his sides to keep from reaching for her. "You still blame me for leaving, even now?"

"No," she breathed, unable to find her voice as she admitted the truth. Tears burned in her eyes, and blinking rapidly, she turned her face away, whispering, "But I don't know how to make you love me, either."

His face fell. He started toward her. "Faith, please—"

"Dunwich." Her father's deep voice stopped him in mid-step. "My daughter does not want to marry you, and I will not force her to. As she said, no one else is aware of what happened between you two this evening, and we will keep it that way." He slid an inscrutable glance at Faith, and her throat tightened with both anguish and relief. "So I think it would be best if you leave in the morning." He paused, his gaze swinging back to Stephen. His voice was ice as he ordered, "And do not come back here nor attempt to contact her again."

The two men stared at each other like adversaries, the tension between them so thick that the room pulsed with it, like a crackling electricity. Faith had never seen anyone stand up to her father like this before, and uneasiness spun through her, twisting her belly into knots. The two men she loved most in the world, now at odds because of her...She didn't dare utter a word, not without breaking down completely in desolate sobs.

"Very well." Stephen drew himself up straight, his shoulders stiff and commanding, even though he'd lost this battle. "I have business in London. Let that be my excuse to the other guests for why I've left the party early. I'll be off after I say goodbye to my parents."

"Of course," Papa agreed quietly.

Stephen bowed to her mother and nodded to her father, then paused as he passed Faith on his way toward the door. "I'll leave tomorrow as asked because I don't want to cause problems between our families," he told her. "But I *will* be back for you, Faith. And I will marry you. Count on it."

He caught her gaze and held it while he bowed to her, a silent promise held in those blue depths. Then he strode from the room.

For several long moments, neither Faith nor her parents moved, and despite Stephen's departure, the tension remained. As thick as fog and made worse with each silent second that ticked past.

Faith lowered her tear-blurred gaze back to the rug while her heart pounded a painful beat in her chest. She was right to refuse him, she knew it. So why was the pain so unbearable?

"Do you love him, dear?" her mother asked gently, breaking the deafening silence.

"Yes," she admitted in a choking breath, the single word tearing from her.

"Then why don't you want to marry him?" Papa demanded, exasperation heavy in his voice.

"I didn't say I didn't want to. I said I *wouldn't* marry him." She lifted her face and swiped her hand at her eyes. Leave it to Papa to come down on the side of propriety and Mama to come down on the side of love. But who was on her side?

"Oh, Faith." With a frown of concern, her mother came to her and cupped her face in her hands. She placed a kiss on her forehead and murmured, "It's all so terrible, isn't it, how we can't control our hearts?"

She squeezed her eyes shut and nodded, unable to speak for fear of loosening a flood of uncontrollable sobs.

Mama wiped tenderly at her tear-streaked cheeks. "There's simply no controlling who we love, is there? We always fall for the worst people in the world."

From across the room, Papa cleared his throat.

"I didn't mean you, darling," she clarified over her shoulder.

His lips twisted wryly. "Of course not."

Faith's heart tugged for her parents. They truly loved each other, as deeply now as they did the day they wed. Theirs was the sort of marriage she wanted. A true love match in every way, one in which she could always trust her husband to love and care for her and their children, to always be there for her. She would never settle for less. And she simply couldn't be certain that Stephen was that man.

"Why don't you go to your room now and try to sleep?" her mother said gently. "We'll talk about this in the morning."

Faith shook her head. "There's nothing more to discuss."

"So be it," Mama said gently. "In the morning, then, we'll talk about how there's nothing more to discuss."

Her shoulders sagged. Her mother was only trying to help, but she knew what her parents didn't—she would never change her mind and marry Stephen.

"Good night." She gave her mother a kiss on the cheek, then dutifully crossed the room to place a kiss on Papa's. But he stiffened as she did so, and she knew it would be a long time before she regained his trust.

Faith silently left the room.

The door closed, and Edward Westover blew out a harsh breath as he leaned over his desk on his hands. "Dunwich," he muttered with a shake of his head. "Of all the men for Faith to fall in love with...*him*."

With a soft smile, Kate returned to his side and ran her hands soothingly over his shoulders, kneading the tightly knotted muscles. "And she does love him, you know. It's obvious in every inch of her."

"That's what frightens me." He grimaced. "But does he love her?"

"Of course he does. The way he looked at her when they danced, the way he spoke to her just now..." She smiled knowingly. "And if he's willing to stand up to you like that, then he must be in love." She placed a kiss against his cheek and said softly, "It's the tough soldiers who always fall the

134

hardest. Trust me, I know."

His dubious expression melted into exasperation. He sank down into his chair and tugged her onto his lap, his arms wrapping around her. "She's challenging, independent...selfless to a fault."

Kate smiled. "Would you have wanted her to be any other way?"

Conceding that his wife was right, he answered instead, "She's never defied us before. That's his influence on her."

"No, darling. That's *your* influence." Kate ran her fingertips lovingly through the gray hair at his temple. "Independent, strong, stubborn...She is her father's daughter." She traced her fingertip along his jaw, enjoying the scratch of midnight stubble. "But she'll marry him, I have no doubt." She crooked a brow. "Of course, she'll also make him grovel for embarrassing her by letting them get caught."

He gave a low chortle. "Did you see the way he jumped when we found them? The look on his face—"

"The look on *yours*!" Kate countered, laughing as she wrapped her arms around his shoulders and buried her face against his neck.

She closed her eyes and let the warmth and strength of his arms seep into her, along with the love he carried for her and the passion they still shared, even after two and half decades of marriage and five children. What she wished most for all her children was a marriage as wonderful as the one she shared with Edward.

His laughter faded, and he commented grimly, "He's not good enough for her."

"Darling," she reminded him patiently, "he was born a marquess."

Then she kissed him before he could say anything more.

Chapter Eight

Faith picked a chrysanthemum and sank onto the nearby bench. The afternoon was growing late, and soon she'd have to go inside for tea with the ladies. But for now, she was content to be alone in the garden, alone with her misery and confusion.

As Papa had requested, Stephen left that morning. He'd stayed just long enough to speak to his parents at breakfast, then quietly stepped into his carriage and left for London. Faith had no idea what he'd said to them or what excuses he made for leaving the party early, but now Lady Emily beamed a bright and happy smile at her whenever Faith walked into the room. So to avoid all awkward conversations, Faith had escaped the house for the gardens.

With a heavy sigh, she plucked at the tiny petals. If only it were that easy to escape love.

Oh yes, she'd fallen in love with Stephen. She'd

accepted that, although acceptance didn't make the situation any easier or alleviate her fears of being hurt again. After all, she'd loved him before, too, and the wounding he'd given her had nearly undone her.

But for him to return to her like this, whispering apologies and promises of a future just when she'd finally moved on...How could she be confident that the rogue he'd been was truly gone forever and that he wouldn't revert to his old ways? All she had was his word, and she knew firsthand how little his word had been worth.

Confusion and exasperation rioted inside her until she didn't know what to believe or think, didn't have anything about him that her heart could cling to with certainty. Worse—the romance of the carefully planned picnic, all the flattery, all the kisses he'd so easily taken from her in an attempt to manipulate her...*That* was purely the old Stephen, a man who cared about nothing but getting whatever he wanted. His goals might have changed from four years ago, but his methods of pursuing them remained the same.

And if that hadn't changed about him, how could she believe that he'd changed where it mattered most, in his commitments and resolve? Because she knew that if she pledged her life to him, only for him to fall back into old ways, he would not simply break her heart but shatter it beyond all repair.

She squeezed her eyes shut. Oh, she couldn't bear it!

"Faith?"

She wiped at her eyes to erase any tears which might be visible and forced a smile as her mother approached. "Yes, Mama."

"You've been gone from the house for a good while." Her mother sat beside her on the bench and handed her a handkerchief from her sleeve. "Are you all right?"

"I will be." Many years from now, when she was old and gray and had finally stopped loving Stephen Crenshaw.

Mama squeezed her hand. "Love is never easy, is it?"

Easy? She nearly laughed despite her heartache. For her, love was proving downright impossible.

Mama paused and lowered her voice. "Is it the gossip about Mrs. Halstead that's causing you such distress?"

"No." And it truly wasn't. Those rumors would be quelled if they married and Mary Halstead relocated away from Elmhurst Park.

"Well, that's good, then," her mother assured her soothingly. She asked gently, "Does Stephen make you happy?"

"No...yes...oh, I don't know!" She groaned and hung her head in her hands.

"To be that confused about a man, it must be love."

Mama smiled knowingly and slipped her arm around her shoulders. "And I think he loves you, too, a great deal."

"No," she whispered sadly, her heart full of doubt, "he doesn't."

"You're underestimating him and the man he's become."

"He's the same man he's always been," she answered miserably.

"What makes you think that?"

She drew a deep breath and confided, "When he asked me to marry him, it was so romantic and perfect...Everything I'd always wanted, everything I used to dream about."

"That's wonderful." When Faith didn't agree, Mama's smile faded into a worried frown. "Isn't it?"

With a grimace, Faith dabbed at her eyes with the handkerchief and shook her head. "It was all pretense. He used empty flattery and promises to try to manipulate me, just as he always used to do. He didn't even realize that he was doing it." Her heart thumped hard against her ribs as she admitted, "It's the same as before, when he would use women to get whatever he wanted. But now he's willing to use *me* to gain the respectability and acceptance into society he didn't have before."

"What did he say when you told him of your

concerns?"

"He assured me that he changed, that he would never intentionally hurt me again." She wrung the handkerchief in her fingers. "The worst part is that I'm certain *he* believes he's changed. But what if he's wrong? What proof do I have that he won't turn back into the scoundrel he once was?"

"Oh my darling." Mama hugged her close. "He told you that he's changed, and you need to believe in that." She placed a tender kiss on Faith's forehead. "And in him."

Her chest ached hollow with misery. "But if I can't? Do I marry him anyway when my heart is filled with doubts?"

"No," her mother confirmed with a sigh, "you do not."

She pulled away and sat back, wrapping her shawl around her shoulders against the chilly fall air. "Then I won't marry him. And you and Papa can be assured that—"

A clatter went up from the stables, followed by the sounds of shouts and horse hooves on the gravel.

"What on earth...?" Her mother stood, and the two women hurried out of the garden toward the stables.

A messenger dismounted and tossed the reins to one of the stable boys. He exchanged words with a groom, who nodded, then answered by pointing at Faith and her mother. He strode toward them.

"Ma'am." Removing his hat, he gave a nod to her

mother, then one to her. "Miss. I've come from Elmhurst Park. I have an urgent message for the Marquess of Dunwich."

Her mother stiffened. "I'm Katherine Westover, Duchess of Strathmore."

"Your Grace." The man dropped into a belated bow.

"The marquess is one of our guests. What does this business regard?"

"One of his tenants has taken ill, ma'am. Mrs. Mary Halstead has come down with fever."

Faith's heart somersaulted with dread.

"Mrs. Olsen, our housekeeper, sent me to fetch him. If you could tell me, where might I find him?"

"I am afraid that the marquess left Hartsfield this morning for London," her mother explained. "You'll need to ride on to Dunwich House in Mayfair. Go inside the stables and talk to Masters, our head groom. Tell him that I have authorized you to be given a fresh horse and a sovereign for your trouble." She paused to punctuate the importance of her order. "Ride through the night if you can. It's urgent that you reach the marquess as soon as possible."

"Yes, ma'am." With a hurried bow, he strode inside the stables.

As soon as the man was out of earshot, Faith whispered around the knot tightening in her throat, "Fever?"

Her mother nodded, her lips pressing into a troubled line. "And it must be severe if Mrs. Olsen sent a messenger after Stephen."

"What can we do?" Faith's chest squeezed with equal parts sympathy and concern, not just for Mary but for Stephen as well. He already blamed himself for her situation. If she were ill, her life in danger..."He'll be devastated if anything happens to her. We have to help."

"I've sent the man on to London," her mother replied.

"An entire day's ride away!" If the messenger didn't catch up with him along the road, two days would pass before Stephen would receive the message and reach Elmhurst. "It might be too late."

"I know," Mama whispered with a sense of helplessness, and Faith could see how it tore at her heart not to be able to do anything to help someone in need. "And with Elmhurst only a few hours away."

"He could have ridden there and back in the time since he left this morning," Faith finished, feeling the same helplessness as her mother. Worse, because she was also alarmed for Stephen.

"There's nothing we can do," her mother said quietly.

But Faith heard that tone in her voice, the one that said Mama wanted to be talked out of believing that. "We can go to Elmhurst ourselves and help her."

Mama shook her head. "She's not our concern."

"She matters to Stephen, so she *is* my concern," Faith countered. "You can help her, Mama. I know you can."

She shook her head. "There will be a doctor at Elmhurst to attend her."

"Only a country doctor, most likely," Faith said carefully, knowing exactly where to strike to hit her mother's heart. "Who knows what kind of superstitions he might believe in? He might even make her condition worse."

Mama hesitated, uncertainty darkening her face.

"She has a child," she barely breathed the words, afraid to utter her worst fears aloud. "If he should come down with the fever, as well? If he dies?"

Mama's shoulders sagged. "All right," she acquiesced, "we'll go. But only to check on her and make certain she's under proper care. Then we return immediately, understand?"

Her heart leapt into her throat as she kissed her cheek. "Thank you, Mama!"

"Don't thank me yet," she scolded with a grimace. "We're going to have to tell your father." Mama arched a brow and clarified, "*You* are going to tell him."

Faith took a deep breath of resolve. Facing Papa certainly wouldn't be easy, not after what happened last night. But she knew in her heart that helping Mary

Halstead was the right thing to do. "I know."

Then she hurried into the stable to ask Masters to ready the carriage.

*****

Three hours later, the carriage reached Elmhurst Park just as the sun was setting. As Faith peered out the window, what greeted them was nothing like she expected.

Always before, Stephen had never cared about the estate, viewing Elmhurst as just another burden. One that represented what he loathed most about his life as a peer, trapping him into a life of responsibility and expectation. The last she'd heard anything about Elmhurst had been rumors of how neglected it had become. How a series of bad land agents had left the estate buildings and roads in disrepair, the farms untended, the fences and walls falling down...There had been grumblings from the tenants themselves about the absent marquess and how he simply didn't care about them, and the constant turnover of staff at the manor house and stables only added to the troubles. None of that surprised her. It was exactly what she'd expected from Stephen.

But the estate Faith now saw passing beyond the window looked nothing like that.

The buildings had been freshly whitewashed, the roads and bridges all repaired. The farms were filled with crops in well-tended fields, and the animals were kept safely within mended fences and walls. The entire estate had been transformed from the disarray of the past. Was this Stephen's doing? It had to be...and not just short-term fixes either to pretty it up but time-consuming and costly repairs that said he planned on returning Elmhurst to the grand estate it had once been. The same estate that he would leave as a legacy to his heirs and the generations after him.

Confusion churned inside her. Had she been wrong about him? If he could make this kind of long-term commitment to the estate, then could he make the same kind of commitment to her as his wife?

She simply didn't know.

They stopped at the manor house only long enough to speak to Mrs. Olsen. The housekeeper gave them directions to the cottage where Mary Halstead was living and confirmed that the physician had been called last night. The man had finally arrived that morning shortly before noon, tended to her for a few minutes, then left. He hadn't been back since. Her mother muttered a string of opinions beneath her breath about old physicians and what they could do with their leeches and physic all the way back to the carriage and across the estate to the cottage.

Yet it wasn't a cottage that greeted them but what must have once been a former residence for a county squire before the estate subsumed it. With at least twenty rooms sitting nestled behind tall gables reaching into the darkening sky, the old Tudor house was an amalgamation of stone, timber, and waddle and daub fronting a garden. If Stephen had placed Mary Halstead and her son here, then he'd taken his commitment to them seriously.

All the windows were dark, except for the soft glow of a lamp from a window on the first floor. The darkness sent a cold foreboding creeping into Faith's bones as she stepped down from the carriage. If they were too late, if the worst had already happened—oh how would Stephen bear it?

"Remain here in front, John, in case you're needed," her mother ordered the coachman. Then she gestured for the tiger. "You'll come with us, Marcus."

He grimly tugged at the brim of his hat and followed them to the house. He pounded the iron knocker against the door, then stepped aside.

A few minutes later, the door opened. A girl who couldn't have been more than fifteen or sixteen peered out at them from the light of a candle stub. She looked curiously from Kate Westover to Faith to the uniformed groom behind them. "What do ye all want?"

"We're here to tend to Mary Halstead," Mama

announced. "We received a message from Mrs. Olsen that she'd come down with fever."

The girl's shoulders sagged as a look of relief crossed her tired face. "Oh thank the heavens!" She stepped back and held the door open wide. "This way."

In the dim candlelight, she led them up the stairs and down the hall. The house was silent, dark, and cold.

"I put her up here in the last bedroom," the girl explained, " 'cause ev'ryone knows that fever likes them low places."

"Yes, everyone knows that," her mother repeated in a mutter that Faith recognized as one of suppressed frustration, the same tone she'd used last month when one of the farmers sought to cut the pain of his wife's childbirth by putting an ax beneath the bed. "Who are you?"

"Polly, ma'am. The maid o' all work."

"Where are the housekeeper and other servants?" Faith interjected. She'd not noticed another person in the dark house.

"Ain't none here, miss, 'cept for Mrs. Bailey, who keeps the kitchens and cooks for us. And me, o' course."

Her mother frowned. "Surely his lordship provided a manservant or footman for a house this large."

"Oh yes, ma'am!" She nodded earnestly. "He did. His lordship has been real good an' kind to Mrs. Halstead—to all o' us at Elmhurst, since he returned."

Another pang of doubt stabbed Faith's chest about what to believe about him. Stephen was good and kind to the servants, right down to the lowest maid? The man she knew before had never paid any mind to his staff or tenants at all.

Polly stopped outside the last door. "But when the fever hit, Mrs. Bailey thought 'twas best to send 'em away, along wi' th' other maid." She bit her lip. "Yer angels to come here. Thank heavens Dr. Howston sent ye." She blinked as tears of fatigue and worry gathered in her tired eyes. "I didn't know what to do."

"Dr. Howston did *not* send us." Her mother's mouth tightened. "And apparently *he* didn't know what to do either."

She reached past the maid for the door and entered the room.

The stench of sickness caught Faith unprepared. She nearly gagged, her hand flying to cover her nose and mouth. But her mother hurried forward toward the bed, her years of experience tending to the sick in the villages and serving on the boards of hospitals in London had left her unsurprised by what greeted them. Yet the emotion in her glistening eyes showed her concern.

Mary Halstead lay on the bed. Beads of perspiration covered her red skin, and her dark hair hung tangled around her shoulders from tossing in troubled half-consciousness. Her face and lips were so pale as to be nearly white above the lace-edged neckline of her long-sleeved night rail. Her lips moved wordlessly in some fever-triggered hallucination, and she clutched at the covers as if clinging on for dear life.

Her mother pushed up Mary's sleeve and bit back a muttered curse.

"Dr. Howston bled her, ma'am," Polly offered helpfully, hesitantly approaching the foot of the bed.

"So I see."

"He said them leeches suck the illness from th' body, that they remove poisoned blood an' disrupt the fever." When her mother picked up one of the vials on the bedside table, the maid added, "Quinine pills, ma'am."

She set them down and reached for the second vial. "Along with calomel. She's been purged, too, then?"

"Yes. After the bleeding, to make certain all th' poison in her was got rid of." The maid's voice took on an air of knowing authority and a hint of pride. "When she first came down wi' the fever, I gave her some rhubarb root I'd prepared myself to purge her then. Dr. Howston said I most likely saved her life."

"Good to know," Mama muttered as she placed her hand on Mary's forehead to gauge her temperature. "Because Dr. Howston most likely nearly ended it."

The maid's eyes grew round. "Ma'am?"

"Where's the child?" Faith interjected, before Mama could say anything to make the poor girl feel worse. "The marquess said she has a son."

"In the nursery upstairs, ma'am. Mrs. Bailey's watchin' over him."

Mama solemnly met Faith's gaze. "Go fetch him and Mrs. Bailey, but keep both of them out in the hallway, all right?"

"Yes, Mama."

Faith snatched up Polly's candle stub and hurried up to the nursery on the second floor. The child, who was no more than a year old, lay sleeping in his crib, while Mrs. Bailey snored from the chair beside him. Faith roused her, then took the sleeping toddler into her arms and carried him downstairs.

By the time she returned to the room, with the still-sleepy cook at her heels, her mother had already set the tiger off to fetch a bucket of water, stripped the covers from Mary's body and was working on removing the night rail. But she'd also gotten caught up in an argument with Polly, who kept pulling the gown back into place.

"Ventilation is key," her mother lectured, giving up on the night rail—for now—and moving to throw open the window to let out the stench of sickness and let in the cool evening air.

"Oh no, ma'am, you mustn't!" Polly shrieked and rushed to the window to try to yank it closed.

Mama pushed the second window open, and Faith thought Polly might have apoplexy right there on the sash. "Don't you ever open your windows?"

"Not at night, ma'am. Night air kills! Ever'one knows 'tis true."

"Not everyone." While Polly was still fretting over the windows, her mother returned to stripping off the night rail until Mary lay naked on the bed, giving Polly a whole new set of worries. "But you open your windows during the day?"

"Of course." Polly pulled the top sheet over Mary's body to cover her, and thankfully for the young maid's state of mind, Mama let it stay.

"And when the sun goes behind a cloud, do you rush to close all the windows?"

"No," Polly answered uncertainly, wary about where the duchess was leading her.

"Why not, if the sun's not shining then? So logically a lack of sunshine has nothing to do with the quality of the air. Now, fetch a stack of sheets from the linen."

"Ma'am?" Polly was still reeling under the theory of night air being no worse than day air.

"We're going to soak the sheets in water and cover her

with them. We've got to bring down the fever or she'll burn to death." Just then the tiger carried the bucket of water past Faith and into the room. "Marcus, have John drive you back to the manor house and tell Mrs. Olsen that I need several buckets of ice. I'm certain the estate has an ice house."

So was Faith, knowing the wealth of Elmhurst Park. Although this late in the year, she wasn't certain there would be any ice left, no matter how well Stephen had repaired the estate.

When the tiger hurried out, Mama turned on Polly. "Sheets, girl—go!"

Polly jumped and ran from the room. Then Mama came out to the hall to check the boy, still safely held in Faith's arms. He had woken up amid all the activity and was now wailing at the top of his lungs.

"Go ahead and scream all you want, little one," Mama cooed as she took him from Faith. "That means you're strong and healthy, with no sign of fever. And I mean to keep you that way." She glanced at the older woman. "You're Mrs. Bailey, I gather?"

She nodded with bewilderment. "Yes, ma'am."

"Have you been in this room since Mrs. Halstead came down with the fever?"

"No, ma'am." She glanced into the room, at the woman lying so fitfully on the bed. "I've been keeping the boy clear o' the fever."

"Good. Then go downstairs to the kitchen and make up a clear broth." She handed the toddler to the cook. "When the coach returns, ask Marcus to bring up the broth and John to drive you to the manor house. I want you and the boy to stay there."

"Yes, ma'am." The woman hurried away toward the back stairs, murmuring softly to the toddler to try to stop his tears, but his cries continued all the way down the stairs and into the basement.

Then Mama pulled Faith into her arms and hugged her tightly for several long moments, whispering her thanks to God and fate that her own family was healthy, before releasing her and returning to the bedside.

She snatched up the vial of calomel and threw it out the window.

"No more purging," she announced as she wiped her hands. "And no more leeches."

"And no more Dr. Howston," Faith mumbled, arching a brow.

"As I said, no more leeches," her mother repeated as she reached into the little bag she'd carried with her all the way from Hartsfield, where she kept her medicines and bandages. The same bag that Papa had tried unsuccessfully for years to convince her to abandon, only to finally give in five years ago and buy her a new leather case to replace the old one she'd had since before they'd married. Faith never knew her mother to travel without it, and it was always kept in a special place in the front hall of both Hartsfield Park and Brambly House, ready to be snatched up at a moment's notice.

Mama withdrew a small jar and a tiny earthenware mug. "Nitrous acid vapor," she explained as she made up the mixture, still clinging to the hope that Faith would turn away from caring for animals and take up her work with people. "Half an ounce of vitriolic acid, heated." She held the mug over the lamp on the bedside table. "Add one ounce of powdered niter, a little at a time to the warm acid."

As she added the second ingredient, red fumes rose from the mug. Then she walked around the room, waving the mug to fill the air with its pungent odor.

Faith coughed and covered her nose.

Mama scrunched up her own nose and held the cup away from her. "It stinks like the dickens, but it will help her breathe more easily."

Polly scurried into the room with her arms filled with what looked like every sheet from the house's linen supply, along with a few stolen from the guestrooms for good measure. With Faith and Polly helping, her mother dunked the sheets into the bucket, soaking them with cool water, then spread the wet sheets across Mary's feverish body.

Mama handed the empty bucket to Polly. "Go fetch more water."

Polly left to do as ordered, and Faith wondered if the little maid now reconsidered her gratitude at their arrival.

But her mother's attentions seemed to be helping. Beneath the layer of wet sheets, Mary ceased her tossing and lay still. Her lips stopped moving, and a long sigh poured from her.

"Will she be all right?" Faith whispered.

"We'll know in the morning. We'll keep her cool tonight and try to break the fever," Mama said quietly as she sat on the chair beside the bed and placed a wet cloth over Mary's forehead. "Wet sheets first, then ice if we must. We'll also try to get her to drink some broth to keep her strength up if she becomes lucid."

"And...?" Faith asked, afraid to put voice to her deepest fears. *And if she doesn't become lucid? If the fever doesn't break?*

"And we pray."

Chapter Nine

Faith heard the long case clock in the entryway strike the hour, its dull chimes echoing through the silent house. Midnight. The second one she'd spent here. Fighting back an exhausted yawn, she rose from the chair and stretched out her cramped legs and stiff back.

She looked down at the woman in the bed. Mary was better than when they'd arrived last night, but she was still in the throes of illness. After continually covering her in wet sheets, and once going so far as to cover her in a thin layer of ice when Mama feared the worst just before dawn, her temperature had finally eased.

By sunset, her condition had improved enough that Faith insisted Mama go the manor house so that she could have a good night's rest in comfort and send Papa a message that they were going to be away longer than expected. Even in her fatigue, though, Mama had initially refused. It was only when Faith insisted that she check on Jeremy and the others at the house that Mama finally relented, promising to return first thing in the morning. Then Faith sent Polly to bed in the room across the hall to catch her own much-needed sleep and sat down for a long night's vigil.

Yet Mary was still insensible, never becoming completely lucid, and in her feverish confusion, she'd mumbled Stephen's name and asked for her son. Whenever she did, Faith held her hand and spoke to her softly, reassuring her that Jeremy was safe and that Stephen was on his way.

"Daniel..." Mary murmured across parched lips. "Daniel..."

Not knowing what to say to bring her comfort, Faith silently squeezed her hand, holding it until Mary fell back to sleep.

That name, spoken with so much grief and utter desolation even in her delirium, sent an icy chill spiraling down Faith's spine. To have so desperately loved him, yet every day seeing his son and being reminded of the love she'd lost...Faith didn't think she could have borne it.

But wasn't that exactly what was happening with her and Stephen, losing the love and future she could have had with him? Except that Stephen hadn't been ripped away from her; she'd pushed him away herself. And for what—to save her heart from being broken again? Yet every hour that ticked past brought with it an ache of loss so intense that she was certain her heart had once more shattered, this time at her own cowardly hands.

Oh, she was a fool! One who was desperately trying to convince herself that she'd made the right decision in rejecting his proposal. Except that she wasn't certain at all anymore. Being here at Elmhurst Park, seeing with her own eyes the changes he'd made in his life, and hearing from Polly story after story about the good man he'd become, it all made her doubt her conviction that he was still the same scoundrel he'd always been.

Men *could* change, couldn't they? Papa said they did, and that war changed them most of all. Could Stephen have changed enough to no longer be the man who had so deeply wounded her before? No longer a heartless rake who bedded every willing woman he came across but now a man who would give his heart and body only to her?

Unable to sit still another moment, she rose to her feet and paced the room. She was exhausted— No, she was past exhaustion, unable to rest even while Mary slept. Doing her best to fight down both the physical fatigue and the emotions clawing at her insides, she decided to keep herself busy by making up another mug of red vapor, carefully measuring the ingredients as Mama had shown her—

The clamor of heavy footsteps broke the silence.

"Mary!" Stephen's voice boomed through the house as he raced up the stairs and down the hall.

The cup fell from her hand and spilled onto the floor as Faith's heart leapt into her throat.

He stopped in the doorway, and his eyes landed on the woman's limp figure in the bed for only a moment before darting to Faith. Bewilderment clouded his face to find her there, then vanished beneath an expression of deep worry as he slowly entered the room. Crossing stiffly to the bed, he sat on the wooden chair and reached for Mary's hand. With a frown, he touched her cheek, and Faith was certain he could feel the fever that still gripped her.

"Mary...Mary, it's Stephen," he said gently. He moved his hand to her forehead and frowned with deep concern. "I'm here. Can you hear me? I'm going to take care of you, I promise. Mary?"

There was no response from her. He blew out a deep breath and released her hand to sit back in the chair.

Then he turned in the chair, lifting his exhausted gaze to Faith. "How is she?" His eyes were grim. "The truth."

"Better," Faith answered, remaining on the far side of the room when what she wanted to do was rush into his arms and beg his forgiveness. "She's resting more quietly now, but the fever hasn't yet broken."

He nodded with bleak understanding. "Is the physician here?"

"No." She picked up the mug, then set it aside and nervously wiped her hands on a towel. "But Mama's been attending her since last night."

"Where's Jeremy?" Dread laced his voice. "Is he ill, too?"

Her chest tightened at his concern for the boy. If he could care this much about a child who wasn't even his..."He's well." She twisted her hands in the towel to keep from reaching for him. "He's at the manor house with Mama."

His shoulders drooped with relief, and he rubbed at his forehead. "I came straight here as soon as I received the message. I didn't stop at the house." Fatigue showed in every inch of him as he heaved out a tired breath. "I was afraid that I might have already been too late."

"I know," she said softly, hot tears blurring her eyes at his compassion. How could she have ever doubted him? "But you're here now. That's all that matters."

She looked away so he couldn't see the guilty self-recrimination playing across her face. She'd been such a goose! She knew now how much he'd changed, had seen it with her own eyes in what he'd done with the estate...in the weariness and worry she saw in him now for Mary and her son. He wasn't that same boy who had once shattered her heart.

He was now the man she loved and always would.

And she'd ruined it all by refusing him. She wouldn't blame him if he hated her for it.

"But that's not all." he said quietly. He stood and walked slowly toward her, then rested his palm against her cheek and lifted her face until she looked at him. "Why are *you* here?"

She swallowed hard and admitted in a whisper, "Because I know how important she is to you."

He murmured, "So are you."

Beneath the exhaustion of the past two days and her own foolishness of the past four years, she was unable to stop a tear from falling down her cheek.

"I care about you, Faith. I would never do anything to hurt you." His face filled with concern for her, and he gently wiped away the tear with his thumb. "Please believe that."

She couldn't hold back the flood of tears at his tender words. "I'm so sorry, Stephen," she choked out between sobs, unable to keep down the swelling emotions inside her chest a moment longer. "I'm so sorry for not believing you...for doubting you..."

He stared at her, saying nothing. The unbearable silence was broken only by the merciless pounding of her heart, each beat a pained pang of dread and loss.

"If you can find it in your heart, please forgive me." She pressed her hand against her chest, as if she could physically tamp down the rising fear that she'd lost him before he was ever truly hers. She whispered so softly that the words were barely more than a breath, "If you care about me at all..."

"I do, more than you know." He cupped her face in his hands and lowered his head to touch his lips tenderly to hers. "But I can't forgive you when—"

"Miss! I heard a noise!" Polly ran into the room, and Stephen straightened immediately.

The young maid stopped short and stared at him. Her face blossomed into a bright smile of relief as she lowered into an awkward curtsy.

"Your lordship!" Then she saw Faith and frowned at her tears. "Miss?"

Faith pulled back from him. As she turned away, she swiped at her tears and saw Stephen's concern for her darken his face. But he hadn't forgiven her, and once more her heart was breaking.

"Polly," Stephen acknowledged with a nod at the young maid. "Thank you for being here."

"Good to have yer lordship returned, sir." Polly hurried forward to the bedside to check on Mary. "We've been our wits' ends. Dr. Howston tended to her yesterday morning. I was watchin' her an' Mrs. Bailey was keepin' Jeremy, when Lady Faith an' Her Grace arrived. Saved her life, they did."

At the compliment, Faith reached within herself to somehow keep her dignity when what she wanted to do was tuck herself into a little ball until the pain faded. Until she could sort through all the emotions churning inside her and somehow salvage the pieces of her heart.

"What do we do next, miss?" Polly looked at her expectantly, as if she held all of life's answers in the palm of her hand. Oh, the furthest thing from the truth!

She shook her head, her vision blurring with hot tears. "I can't...I just *can't*..." She swallowed hard, choking back the roiling knot of emotions rising to the surface and the sheer exhaustion sweeping over her. "Please tend to Mrs. Halstead," she forced out the pleading order around the suffocating knot in her throat. "I need air. I need to breathe and—"

She fled from the room, plunging herself into the dark hall and hurrying through the silent shadows. Her breath came hard and fast and shallow, her heart beating frantically. She had no idea where she was going, only that she needed to flee and put as much distance between herself and Stephen as possible.

Reaching the end of the hall, she flung open the door of a guestroom and ran inside. Her hands grabbed for the back of a chair, and she clung to it, as if it were the only thing in the world keeping her from falling away. She'd been such a fool! And now everything between them was irreparably destroyed.

"Faith?" he whispered, his deep voice raspy with concern.

She tensed as Stephen stepped into the room with her, then shut the door behind him, locking them together in the shadows.

Oh, why wouldn't he simply leave her be? Didn't he realize how torturous it was for her to be in the same room with him, knowing that she'd ruined everything between them? She hadn't trusted him, had been unwilling to believe that he'd changed—

Now that she knew the truth, it was too late.

"Please leave," she whispered, unable to find her voice beneath the pain pulsing inside her and the realization of all she'd lost.

"I won't do that," he assured her as he forward. "You're upset, and I care too much about you to let you cry alone."

He stopped behind her, not touching yet close enough that she could feel the heat of his body warming hers.

"You care about me?" she whispered, the breathless words shattering the darkness. She didn't dare hope...

"Very much."

She squeezed her eyes shut against the tears. "But you said you can't...can't forgive me..."

"Because there's nothing to forgive."

A gasp tore from her as she turned to face him. She couldn't believe— "You don't...hate me? After the way I refused you, after all those horrible things I said..."

"I could never hate you, Faith." He slipped his arms around her and pulled her against him, holding her close. "I know how hard my return has been for you." He stroked his hands in small, reassuring circles across her back. "How much I hurt you before, how confused I'm making you now...I'm the one who needs to be forgiven."

A soft sob fell from her lips. Her heart was too full to find any words to express how she felt, how much she loved him. All she could do was tighten her hold around his waist to keep him close. Always.

"I want a life with you, a home, and children." He nuzzled his cheek against her hair, and the affection in that little caress made her tremble. "I promise you that I will be the husband you deserve and that I will be faithful in every way."

Lifting her head from his chest, she rose up on her

tip-toes to brush her lips against his. He closed his eyes against the tenderness of her kiss.

"Faith," he rasped out, "my darling...I've made a mess of things...you, Mary, Jeremy...Daniel."

"It isn't your fault," she whispered against his lips, each word a breath of absolution for both of them. "No one's to blame, certainly not you."

How could the past four years have been anyone's fault? Mama was right. What power did a person truly have over his or her heart? Fools all, to think that emotions could ever be controlled. How well she knew that truth herself! Because if she could have controlled her heart, she never would have fallen in love with Stephen all those years ago, and she wouldn't have tumbled back into love with him once he returned.

But thank God she had.

"I never meant to hurt you," he confessed as he rained tender kisses against her cheek, her jaw, her lips—each one filled with regret, each one leaving her desperate to erase his pain. "I only wanted to make you happy."

With a nervous stutter of her heart, yet undeniably certain of the love she felt for him, she cupped his face in her hands. "Then make me happy," she whispered, touching her lips to his. "Make love to me."

*****

Stephen stared down at her, his heart pounding and his stomach suddenly tying itself into knots. "I do, you know," he murmured as he pulled the pins from her hair.

Her eyes closed as he combed his trembling fingers through her tresses, spreading the soft waves down her back in a silky curtain. "Do what?"

"Love you," he whispered breathlessly.

Her eyes flew open. Stunned, she gazed up at him with parted lips, as if she couldn't believe he'd said it, and that disbelief gnawed at him.

He'd given her so little reason to trust him over the years. But he resolved to prove to her exactly how much he'd changed, how much he needed her to heal his soul. And most of all, how much he loved her. Starting tonight.

"Four years ago, I took you for granted," he continued, "and I was a damned fool not to recognize how much you meant to me or all I'd lost by leaving. Your friendship." He placed a soft kiss against her cheek. "Your caring." Another kiss to the tip of her nose. "Your brilliance and tenderness." Two kisses on her eyelids, and his heart nearly shattered when he tasted the salt tears there. "Your love."

He gently caressed his mouth back and forth across hers. She sighed beneath his kiss, and he knew then that she was finally his. His heart soared with joy.

"When Daniel died and Mary lost her chance at a future with him," he murmured, staring down into her eyes, "I realized how precious life is. And I swore to myself that I'd make everything right. That I'd take care of Mary and protect Daniel's son and his reputation. That I'd find a way to convince you that I'd changed. That I wasn't the same boy I'd been before but a man worthy of you." Nervous uncertainty flared inside him as he searched her face in the shadows. She hadn't yet said..."Do you think you could find it in your heart to love me, Faith?"

"I do love you," she whispered, each word a trembling admission. "I've always loved you."

With a laugh of happiness, he lifted her into his arms and spun her in a circle, then captured her mouth in a kiss that left both of them gasping for breath.

Beneath her eager lips, his laughter turned into a groan of desire. Dear God, how long he'd waited for this, to hear those words fall from her lips and feel the softness of her in his arms, freely giving both the physical love of her body and the healing love of her soul. Faith clung to him, her arms wrapped so tightly around his shoulders that she seemed unwilling to ever let go. Which was perfectly fine with him.

He carried her across the room to the bed. As he laid

her down gently on the mattress, he leaned over to suck at her bottom lip and drew a moaning sigh of pleasure from her that left him shaking so hard that his fingers fumbled to unfasten the row of tiny buttons on her bodice. There was no turning back now. There was only going forward into the future. Together.

He peeled the dress away, then relished in slowly removing each undergarment. As one layer after another dropped away and bared stretches of smooth flesh, he followed along in their wake with his mouth, murmuring continuously against her skin how beautiful she was, how much he loved her...

When only her chemise and stockings remained, he broke a lingering kiss to stand beside the bed and stare down at her. Sweet Lord, she was a vision in the slant of moonlight that fell from the window across the bed. So beautiful, so delicate...so much like an angel that she stole his breath away. She watched him curiously as he removed his clothes and tossed aside the dusty redingote and breeches he'd worn all the way from London, riding straight through to get here, never realizing that Faith would be waiting for him like a wish come true.

He pulled off his boots and dropped them one by one to the floor, followed by his neck cloth and waistcoat. When he pulled his shirt off over his head, baring himself from the waist up and leaving him in only his riding breeches, he heard her catch her breath, and her lips pulled into a soft O of surprise. Her gaze raked over him, and shamelessly, he let her look. She was still innocent, and the thought that she was giving that innocence to him sent his heart racing with both trembling nervousness and selfish pleasure.

Slowly, careful not to make her any more nervous than she already was, he unbuttoned the fall of his breeches and pushed them down and off until he was completely naked. How much could she see in the moonlight and shadows as her gaze traveled over him? He had no idea, but when he crawled back onto the bed with her and stretched his tall body alongside hers, her breath came in shallow pants not from fear but desire.

"You are so beautiful, Faith," he murmured, trailing his hand over her hip and down her leg. When he hooked his fingers beneath the hem of her chemise and gently tugged it upward, she shivered.

"So are you," she whispered breathlessly, her nervous misspeak earning her a low chuckle from him.

"I can't tell you how many times I lay awake in bed and dreamed of being with you." To ease her nervousness when the hem reached the apex of her thighs, he lowered his head to place a distracting kiss against her throat, rewarding him in turn by the delicious beat of her racing pulse against his lips.

"I wish you hadn't," she admitted, her voice a soft ache.

He lifted onto his forearm to stare down into her face, puzzled. "Why not?"

Her eyes lowered to his mouth, not so much because she wanted him to kiss her but to shyly avoid making eye contact. "I'll never live up to your fantasy."

"No," he countered softly, outlining her lips with his fingertip. "You're so much better than I ever imagined."

Before she could argue, he kissed her, this time drinking in her sweetness and stirring up the desire already flaming inside her. When he lifted the chemise the rest of the way up her body and cast it away to the floor, leaving her naked, there was no nervousness between them, no awkwardness. She didn't try to cover herself, not even when he gazed down at her in the moonlight.

"So beautiful," he repeated in an incredulous murmur and drifted his hand over her body, fluttering lightly over her breasts and all the way down to the soft curls guarding her womanhood. "An angel."

He placed a tender kiss on her nipple, then another and another, until it puckered into a hard point. Unable to resist, he closed his lips around it and took a gentle suck.

"Stephen!" she gasped, her hands going to his head.

A low chuckle rose in his throat at her reaction, and he shamelessly took another suck, this time drawing her deeper into his mouth. She moaned and arched her back beneath him, thrusting her breasts toward him.

"So sweet," he mumbled against her breast, her fingers running through the hair at his nape in soft encouragement.

As he suckled his fill of her, his hand caressed her other breast and massaged her fullness beneath his palm. He teased her nipple into a hard point to match the first, then slid his mouth over to claim the same delicious taste of it. She was perfect, warm and soft, so incredibly sweet, and everything about her soothed his pained soul. He'd suspected that she'd be able to heal him the way nothing else could, and as he felt the happiness swell in his chest, he knew he'd been correct. Only Faith, only this sweet joining of bodies and souls with her.

Each plundering kiss against her mouth and each caress of his hands across her breasts made it impossible for her to lie still beneath him. She whimpered softly and shifted her hips against the mattress, and he nearly groaned at the arousal blossoming inside her, so unknown to her that she didn't know how to ask for what her body wanted.

But he knew, and he would happily give her what she craved. He slipped his hand down through the triangle of curls, his fingers sliding into the damp heat of her folds beneath. He stroked against her—

"Stephen," she moaned against his mouth, then tossed all inhibition aside by spreading her thighs and latching onto his tongue with her lips, suckling as sweetly at him as he had at her breasts. He hardened instantly, and all of him ached with a desperate longing to claim her as his.

His Faith. Now and always.

As his fingers caressed against her, arousal flamed inside him with each daring suck of her lips and with each plunge of her tongue inside his mouth to share the wonderful intimacy of their kiss. The intoxicating sounds of her soft mewings and whimpers of need swirled through him and made him long to hear her moan with pleasure and cry out with passion.

Breaking the kiss, he shifted away just far enough to gaze down at her and watch the emotions flittering across her face as he slipped two fingers inside her silky warmth.

"Oh!" She tensed for a moment, then relaxed. She let out a long sigh as he continued to caress inside her in smooth, steady strokes. "Oh my..."

He placed a kiss at her temple. "Does that feel good?"

"Oh heavens...yes...very much," she answered between pants.

"Very much," he repeated with a smile as he watched

her close her eyes against the mounting ache growing inside her, so strongly that he could feel it pulsing against his fingers as he swirled them inside her.

His thumb delved down into her folds to find the tiny nub buried there. He rubbed it lightly, and she responded with a shiver, her sex clenching tight around his fingers and demanding to be brought to release. So tight and warm and slippery...He couldn't believe how much she trusted him, making herself open and vulnerable to him like this. Just as he couldn't believe how beautiful she was. Or how very much he loved her.

"Faith," he whispered and touched her most sensitive spot again, this time pressing down hard enough that a low moan tore from her. Her arms wrapped around his neck to keep him close, and her thighs quivered. "Darling Faith."

He rubbed her again, and a wave of pleasure swept through her in a shuddering release. Her body clenched around his, then she went limp beneath him on the mattress, her lips parting and panting to recapture the breath he'd stolen.

The expression of pure joy on her face nearly undid him. He whispered chokingly around the knot in his throat, "I love you, my darling."

Lifting onto his forearms, he settled himself into the cradle of her spread thighs. All of him shook with emotion and need as he positioned the head of his erection against her, notching himself there as he paused to enjoy another lingering kiss at her heated lips. He would only have this moment once, this first joining with her, and he wanted to savor it, to be able to remember it always.

He whispered, "My Faith...my angel..." *My life.*

With a sigh of longing against her mouth, he lowered his hips and sank inside her.

Faith closed her eyes and held her breath as his warm, hard body so slowly, so lovingly filled hers. She expanded to take him in, her already sensitized womanhood tingling achingly with each patient plunge and retreat. Each caressing stroke of his body went slightly deeper than before, and with each, he placed a reassuring kiss on her lips. Tears gathered at her lashes at the unbelievable tenderness in him. She'd never imagined that being with a man could be like this—

No, it was only because of Stephen. No other man could have made her feel as beautiful and wanted as he did, so feminine and desirable...so *loved.*

He stilled and held himself poised over her. With his eyes squeezed closed, he whispered her name as he lowered his mouth to cover hers. Then he thrust his hips forward and plunged fully inside her.

She gasped at the sharp pinch inside her, and her

body tensed around him at the fleeting pain.

But when Stephen began to move his hips against hers in slow, steady strokes, the discomfort faded, replaced by a tingling ache that grew more and more demanding. The same tingling ache which had engulfed her when he'd caressed her with his fingers, and oh how wonderful that had been! If he could do that to her with just his hand, to think what he could do to her with his body—

Heaven. She rolled back her head and arched herself beneath him.

A growling sound of pleasure tore from his throat. He wrapped his arms tightly around her and began to thrust deep and hard. The same engulfing tension as before sped through her, but this time it was so much more intense than before. It tightened every muscle in her body from the tips of her toes to the top of her head. She rose up against him to meet every thrust, craving more, *needing* more. The throbbing ache inside her swelled like the tightening of a coiled spring—

She broke with a cry. Pleasure rushed through her in a wave. The world around her vanished, until all she knew was the exquisite release pulsing through her and the joy of having his body enveloping hers. When her pulse slowed and the deafening rush of blood pounding in her ears subsided, she felt his lips at her ear whispering over and over how much he loved her.

She could do nothing more than cling to him as he continued to stroke into her, her arms wrapped around his neck and her ankles locked together at the small of his back. As his tempo increased, so did the intensity of their joining, and each thrust now came as a jerky, grinding drive of his hips against hers.

With a low groan, he plunged deep inside her and held himself there for a heartbeat, then with a shudder poured himself inside her. At this new, wholly wonderful sensation of his life's essence flowing into her, a pulse of joy swept through her, and a tear slipped down her cheek.

He rested his forehead against her bare shoulder as he struggled to regain his breath, trembling and covered with perspiration. When he recovered, he placed a tender kiss on her lips. His eyes glistened in the moonlight as they stared down into hers, their bodies still joined below, and their hearts beating fiercely into each other's chest.

"I love you, Faith," he whispered, his mouth so close to hers that she shivered at each warm breath that stirred across her lips. "I'm going to prove to you that I deserve your love, that I will always keep you safe." He kissed her. "And I'm going to spend the rest of my life making you happy."

She blinked away tears of joy and breathed, "You already have."

He kissed her, softly and tenderly, then shifted his weight off her to lie beside her on the bed. She snuggled into his arms, never wanting to leave their warm embrace. When he pulled the coverlet over them, to keep away the chill of the night and tuck them together, she rested her palm against his chest and reveled in the strength of his heart beating beneath her fingertips.

Fate had given them a second chance at love, and the future they would create together would be one of happiness, home, and family.

Family. Her belly tightened. She knew how children were created— "We didn't...take precautions," she whispered, embarrassment heating her cheeks.

He grinned at her. "We certainly did not."

The faint warmth flared into a full-out burning blush. She rested her cheek against his chest to hide her face, afraid he might be able to see her reaction even in the moonlight and know how happy the thought made her that she might have gotten with his child.

"So I guess you'll have to make an honest man of me and marry me, or my reputation will be ruined," he teased with mock solemnity. "I'll never be able to wear white gowns and be presented at court now."

She swatted gently at his shoulder, but he caught her hand and raised it to his lips. He placed a kiss against her palm, then set about sucking on each of her fingertips until she trembled. All the teasing between them vanished.

"You *will* marry me, Faith," he assured her as his lips moved from finger to finger, stirring a new ache between her legs and leaving her to wonder how long they had to wait before they could make love again. "You will be my wife, my marchioness, and the mother of my children." He trailed his mouth down her inner wrist. "And I will always be your dutiful husband. In." He placed a kiss on her forearm. "Every." Another kiss in the crook of her elbow. "Way."

With a sigh of happiness, she rested her cheek against his chest. "In every way," she repeated. A happy smile played at her lips as she whispered, "My husband."

Nervous butterflies danced in her belly when she thought of it. And what they'd just done. It had been absolutely wonderful! Now she knew why her older sisters gazed on their husbands in that dreamy way they did, why her parents insisted that she and her siblings find love matches. Oh, love was divine!

Her heart felt so full that she wondered how it didn't burst. She'd never been happier in her life as she was at that moment, knowing that Stephen loved her. That they would marry and spend the rest of their lives together. *Simply heaven.* They would have to be careful—they weren't married yet, and God help him if either of her parents caught them together. Again. But for this moment, he was completely hers.

Stephen Crenshaw was *finally* hers.

It wasn't the way she would have ever imagined a romance between them playing out, but love had blossomed after all.

They had so much to discuss, not least of which was asking Papa's permission to marry her. Formally this time, the way the duke expected of him. But that could all wait. Right now, she cared about nothing more than simply being with him.

She rested her cheek against his chest, closed her eyes, and drank in the delicious pleasure of being in his arms. Within his embrace, comforted by the lullaby of his heartbeat, Faith slipped into peaceful sleep.

Chapter Ten

Stephen lay in bed and watched Faith sleep. The pre-dawn blues of night faded as the light of sunrise began to spill through the window and play across the delicate features of her face. Her smooth skin and high cheekbones, her red-tinged lashes lying softly closed, her pink lips parted slightly, her hair spilling across the pillow...Dear Lord, even asleep she was beautiful. He could barely believe that she was now truly his to love openly and for the rest of his life, or that this caring, wonderful creature had given herself so freely last night.

They would have to rise and dress soon. The duchess would certainly return early to continue her care of Mary, and he needed to visit the manor house, to inform the staff of his arrival and check on Jeremy.

For now, though, there was no hurry to leave the warmth of the bed.

Yet the yearning inside him was too strong to let her keep sleeping. They would be officially engaged as soon as he was able to speak to the duke, but knowing his mother and hers, even a short engagement would mean weeks of wedding planning and no chance to be alone with Faith. He grimaced. After the way he'd left Hartsfield two days ago, Strathmore would certainly ensure it. Months might pass before she was back in his arms.

But at this moment, they were together, and he didn't want to waste a moment.

He caressed his fingertips across her cheek and whispered her name. She stirred but didn't wake. With a small pang of guilt that he wanted to rouse her when she'd been so exhausted last night—but only a very *small* pang—he traced his thumb along her bottom lip.

Her eyes opened with a light flutter of lashes and a soft inhalation. She stared at him, sleep-dazed and confused, which sent an amused warmth spreading through him. Clearly, she didn't remember yet why she hadn't awoken in her own bedroom at home, or why they were sleeping together in the same bed, still naked beneath the covers—

Then a smile tugged at her lips, and her eyes cleared with a bright sparkle.

"Good morning." He leaned over her to place a kiss against her lips.

"A *very* good morning," she murmured against his mouth as her arm snaked around his neck to pull him closer to her.

He kissed her languidly, savoring the sweet taste of her. As she returned his kiss and relaxed beneath him with a sigh, she ran her fingers through his hair and unwittingly stoked the tingle of arousal slowly building inside him. He smiled against her mouth. He wanted to wake up like this every morning, and soon, he'd be able to do just that.

"Did you sleep well?" she asked.

He slipped his hand beneath the blanket and caressed over her body. "Quite restful." He cupped her breast against his palm, handling her gently, knowing she would still be sore. "Soft mattress," he murmured as his fingers strummed her nipple. It tightened instantly with the memory of what pleasures he could give. "Warm blankets."

"Warm man," she corrected, her breath growing shallow with arousal.

He grinned down at her, happier than he'd ever been in his life. His hand left her breast to roam lower. "Soft woman." Oh so *very* soft and inviting, and for the moment all his to savor. His hand stroked idly against her lower belly, his fingertips brushing tantalizingly against her feminine curls. "And you, love? Did you sleep well?"

"Yes," she sighed, which turned into a low moan when

he stroked between her legs. "Oh yes..."

He watched the pleasure dance across her face as she closed her eyes and held her breath against the intimate caresses he gave her. He didn't want to hurt her by bedding her again so soon, but already she was wet with desire and ready for him. And his body longed for hers.

"Are you too sore?" Concern thickened his voice as he watched for any sign of discomfort on her face as he lightly teased her with his fingertips.

"No," she answered between soft pants. "That feels good."

He groaned. It felt *very* good. Unable to resist, he stroked harder against her, caressing deeper into her slick softness. "And this?"

She gave an answering sound that was half moan, half whimper. And all pleasure. Her hand slipped down between them and folded around his cock, then gave a tentative stroke along his shaft that left him shaking.

"And you?" Another long, slow stroke of her hand, this time much bolder, and he squeezed his eyes shut. Then she asked so softly that he could barely hear her, the innocent question in complete opposition to the wicked way she was pleasuring him, "Are you sore here?" Her thumb caressed over his tip in curious exploration of his body and teased at the tiny slit, where already a drop of wetness gathered. "Or here?"

Losing his restraint, he brought his mouth down hard over hers, capturing her lips in a fierce, open-mouthed kiss that had her arching beneath him—

A knock rapped sharply at the door. "My lord?" More knocking, harder and more insistent as Polly continued to call out for him. "Sir! Wake up, please!"

Faith's eyes grew wide.

He placed his fingertip against her lips in warning to keep quiet, then called out over his shoulder. "I'm awake. What is it?"

"It's Mrs. Halstead, sir. Her fever's broken!"

A long, jerking sigh of relief poured from him. "Thank God."

"She's askin' fer ye, sir. I came to fetch ye."

Faith sucked in a silent breath.

"I need a moment to dress. Go find Lady Faith," he called out with a grinning wink at her. "She's sleeping somewhere downstairs."

"Yes, sir!" The sound of scurrying footsteps drifted away.

"You're terrible," Faith scolded in a whisper.

He arched a brow. "You'd rather she find us together like this?" With a last, lingering kiss, he rolled off her and out of bed. He snatched up his breeches from the floor and yanked them on. "That should buy us a few minutes while she hunts for you." He slipped his shirt over his head. "I'll go to Mary, and you can follow when you've finished dressing."

She sat up and pulled the covers over her body to hide her nakedness. Which was a damned shame, as far as he was concerned. Although if he'd remained here with her looking like that for a minute longer, nothing could have pulled him away.

"You're awfully good at hiding naked women," she commented quietly, wariness darkening her face.

"Don't look at me like that." He dared to play with fire by leaning over the bed. "I might have changed, but I still remember how to be a rake." He pulled down the sheet to bare a single plump breast and placed a kiss on her nipple. When it puckered eagerly beneath his lips, he groaned and murmured with a heavy sigh, "I'm going to miss being a rake."

She swatted at him again. Laughing, he dodged her hand and grabbed up the rest of his clothes from the floor.

Buttoning up his waistcoat, he grinned back at her and reluctantly slipped into the hall.

He was dressed halfway respectable by the time he reached Mary's room, although covered in prickly morning beard and still somewhat dusty from yesterday's ride. He stifled a silly grin. It must be love if Faith found him desirable looking this rumpled and worn.

He paused in the doorway. "Mary?"

She opened her eyes, and his heart skipped. "Stephen," she mumbled, "you're here..."

With a rush of relief, he hurried forward and sat on the chair drawn up to her bedside. He reached for her hand. "Thank God you're better. You had me worried."

She smiled weakly at him. "You weren't the only one."

Footsteps hurried down the hall and into the room. "Sir! I can't find Lady Faith anywhere downstairs."

"How peculiar." He kept his face inscrutable, except for a twitch at his lips. "Did you check in the kitchens?"

Footsteps raced away.

Looking at her with a mix of relief and sympathy, Stephen placed his hand against her forehead, then smiled. She would have a long recovery ahead of her to regain her strength, but now her forehead was cool to the touch and the color had returned to her cheeks.

With a grateful smile, she took his hand and squeezed it, but the gesture which was meant to reassure him of her strength only reinforced how weak she was.

She tried to sit up. "Where's Jeremy?" A panicked worry rose in her voice as she glanced around the room. "Jeremy!"

Stephen took her shoulders and gently put her down

against the pillows. "He's all right. He's at the manor house."

She nodded and eased down, the panic leaving her but not its intensity. "I want to see him."

"You will," he assured her in as soothing a voice as possible. "Soon. But for now, you need to rest and regain your strength."

She blinked rapidly as tears welled in her eyes. "I was so frightened. I kept having nightmares..."

"It was only the fever," he said gently.

She shook her head, tears spiking her lashes. "I thought I was going to die." Her hand tightened around his, and his chest ached that he couldn't help ease her fear. "And I was so terrified. Not for me, but for Jeremy. What would he do if anything happened to me? How would he survive if he lost me, too?"

Too. Along with his father. "He would have me," he rasped hoarsely. "Always."

"Thank you, Stephen," she whispered. "Everything we have is because of you. I don't know what we'll do without you, or how we'll ever repay you."

"You don't have to repay me," he assured her. Then he added quietly, despite the tightening of his chest at the repercussions of what he was offering—"I think you should remain here at Elmhurst and not leave as we'd planned."

She shook her head weakly. "I cannot do that."

Sympathy softened her face. "You need to marry and have children, and the last thing a new marriage needs is scandalous rumors that you're keeping a mistress in your back garden. *If* her father consents to let you marry her at all."

He clenched his jaw at that brutal dose of reality. She was right. As long as Mary remained at Elmhurst, Strathmore would never consent for Faith to marry him. "I don't care about rumors and untruths." Although how he planned on convincing Strathmore to think the same, he had no idea.

"*I* care." She grimaced. "And so will your wife."

"The woman I marry will be strong. She won't let a few rumors bother her." Faith was too strong to let gossip stop her from getting what she wanted. His chest warmed, because finally what she wanted was *him*.

"She might very well not," Mary continued, regret lacing her voice, "but she also doesn't deserve to have what should be the happiest time of her life tarnished because of me."

Guilt tightened his chest. "I won't have you leave, Mary, not when you have no one else to care for you."

"And you can't have us stay either," she whispered, blinking at her tears. "So where will that leave your wife, except caught in the middle? Is that really how you want to start your life together?"

He bit back a frustrated curse. "That isn't at all—"

Her eyes darted to the doorway. Stephen looked up.

Faith stood there, and for several long seconds, none of them moved. His heart pounded. How long had she been there? How much had she overheard? Although judging by the dark frown marring her suddenly pale face, she'd been there long enough to hear far too much.

Forcing a smile, she came forward hesitantly into the room with her hands folded in front of her. God only knew what thoughts were speeding through her mind, if already she was regretting last night and her promise her marry him.

Stephen stood and introduced quietly, "Mary, this is the woman who's been caring for you. Lady Faith Westover. Faith—" He hesitated as she came to his side. "This is Mary Halstead."

Mary sat up and leaned heavily against the pillows. "Thank you for caring for me. I owe you my life."

"It wasn't as desperate as that," Faith answered with a faint smile. An obvious lie meant to make Mary feel better.

"And Jeremy? Did you care for him, too?"

"No, my mother took care of him."

Mary's eyes moved between Stephen and Faith, as if searching for answers. "You know...who I am, then? Stephen's told you?"

"Yes. You're the woman Daniel loved," Faith acknowledged softly. She drew a deep breath and whispered, "I'm so sorry that you lost him."

"Thank you," Mary whispered, unable to find her voice as her eyes glistened with tears.

"Daniel would have been so proud of Jeremy," Faith commented. She sat on the chair beside the bed. "He's a beautiful boy." Her face broke into a proud smile over her son. "He's a handful, but smart."

"I'm looking forward to getting to know him, and you."

"Me, too, my lady."

She smiled gently, and the awkwardness between the two women melted away. "Please...call me Faith."

Stephen watched as they fell into conversation about Jeremy and how rambunctious he was, even for his young age, and how rambunctious Polly was for hers.

With every smile and soft laugh that came from Faith, his chest squeezed tighter around his heart. Unable to remain in the room a moment longer, he walked into the hall and stopped only when he reached the stairs, where he leaned heavily against the banister and drew a deep breath.

Faith and Mary...he'd never realized before exactly how intertwined their lives would become. Oh, he knew that the gossip which surrounded Mary and him would make it difficult for Faith to marry him. But knowing how strong Faith was, he'd focused his determination on gaining her love anyway, believing that he could move Mary away, set her up in the life she would have had if Daniel hadn't died, and send away the rumors right along with her. That whatever gossip lingered after that could be ignored until it vanished completely.

But Faith had been right that day during the pall mall game that simply giving Mary a new home wouldn't be enough to break from the shadow of his misspent youth. How ironic her solution had been—that he needed to marry as well. Yet she'd had no idea that he'd already determined to do just that. With her. He'd thought that had solved their problems. Confident of it enough, in fact, that he'd arranged that picnic in the stables with the sole intention of proposing to her.

He'd been so very wrong. *Solved* their problems? Their troubles were only beginning.

But he knew one thing for certain. Now that Faith was his, he had no intention of *ever* letting her go. No matter what he had to do to ensure that.

*****

When Mary fell into a peaceful sleep, Faith quietly left the room to let her rest and to find Stephen. Last night in his arms, she'd thought that there was still a lot between them to discuss before they could start their new life together. Now a mountain stood between them, and she couldn't see to the other side.

She saw him and stopped. He stood at the top of the stairs, leaning back against the railing as if waiting for her, his arms folded and his gaze staring thoughtfully at the floor. Dressed in the same clothes he'd worn all the way from London, his hair sleep-mussed and stubble darkening his face, she'd never seen him look so disheveled. Or so breathtaking.

Or so troubled.

When he looked up and his eyes softened on her, she came forward and stepped into his embrace, circling her arms around his waist as his own folded around her and held her close.

"Mary's going to be just fine," she told him.

"Thank God," he murmured, his lips resting against her hair. Then he drew in a deep breath, held it for a moment, then said quietly, "She's right, you know. Her presence here will only cause problems for us. But I cannot send her away, not without anyone to look after her."

"No, you cannot," she agreed so softly that her words

were little more than a pained breath.

Her chest squeezed around her heart at the impossible situation they'd been forced into. Mary and Jeremy could never be left without protection and care. They were too vulnerable. This illness proved it. Even if he gave her an allowance and moved them to one of his other properties, they would still need someone to help them. What would Mary do if another fever struck her? Or Jeremy? Who would take care of them then?

"She can stay here," she whispered, despite knowing what it meant for their marriage, how difficult the future would be for them. A man who had spent his life spurning society and the daughter of a duke...Society would simply salivate for the opportunity to make them fall. Yet she didn't care, not as long as she had Stephen's love. "What matters is that we're together. After we marry, everyone will see what a loving marriage we have and—"

"And continue to believe that she's my mistress," he heaved out in a frustrated breath. "Worse, that I'm daring to flaunt her in my wife's face by keeping her here. I would never expose you to that kind of hate-filled gossip." He took her chin and tilted her face up to look at him. His eyes pinned hers. "And the rumors would only increase because we had to elope."

She blinked her tear-blurred eyes, not understanding.

"Why would we elope?"

"Because Strathmore will never give his blessing for you to marry me as long as she's here."

He was right, and the brutality of that truth clawed at her. Papa would never consent to their marriage. But neither would they elope, because she could never defy her father to the point of marrying against his wishes. She would *never* pit the two men she loved most against each other like that. "Then what can we do?"

He grimly shook his head. "I have to make certain Mary and Jeremy are cared for when they leave Elmhurst. There is no other answer."

She pressed herself closer, resting her cheek against his chest and attempting to take comfort in the beating of his heart. Strong. Steady. Pounding hard for her. She'd lain next to him last night in his arms, with her head resting on his chest just like this. The soft sound had brought her such comfort, but now, knowing how much could be lost if fate worked against them, each heartbeat only increased her worry.

She whispered, "I want to help you. We'll find a way out of this." She slipped her hands down his arms to entwine her fingers in his, their hands tightly clasped. "*Together.*"

But his words took her breath away. "Not in this, Faith. I won't ask that of you."

A terrible fear struck her that she was losing him, even now when she stood in his arms. Her anguish was so barely contained that she trembled when he lifted her hand to caress his cheek. "You told Mary that the woman you wed would be strong. So let me be strong for you."

He shook his head. "This is my responsibility. I won't lay this on your shoulders."

The irony squeezed around her heart. How many times since he'd returned had she'd prayed for proof that Stephen had changed, that he was no longer the scapegrace he'd been? That he could be a man whom she could love with every ounce of her soul and heart? Now she had it, irrefutable evidence that he'd become a kind and responsible man—one who would never abandon Mary and her son when they needed him. One who respected her wishes to do the right thing by them, even at the cost of his own happiness. And she *refused* to let him make that sacrifice.

"I *want* to help you," she said gently but with a persistence that came from deep in her soul. He was hers now, and she refused to give him up, especially after last night. Especially now that she knew how much he loved her. "So tell me what we can do...How do we fix this?"

He hesitated. Then, drawing in a deep breath, he murmured, "I have an idea, but it's a long shot."

Wanting to reassure him, she rose up on tip-toes to

kiss him. Only a fleeting touch of their lips, but Faith tasted a world of hope in that kiss. She cupped his face in his hands. "Tell me."

Even as he shared his plans, she wasn't at all certain that it would work. But it *had* to. Because her future with Stephen hung in the balance.

Chapter Eleven

Oldham Village, Lancashire
One Month Later

Stephen knocked on the front door of the Llewellyn family home.

Beside him, Mary clutched Jeremy tightly in the chilly fall air and said nothing in her nervousness. Just as she'd said nothing of worth to him during the five-day ride from Elmhurst Park.

During the past month, he'd sent several letters to the Llewellyns, explaining about Mary and Daniel...and Jeremy. That the boy needed his grandparents. That Mary needed them to help her with him, however they were willing to do. That they owed it to Daniel's memory—and to themselves—to let the child into their lives.

Each of the letters went unanswered.

But he refused to stop trying to persuade them, *couldn't* stop since his future with Faith hung in the balance.

So he'd had Mary write several letters herself, including lengthy descriptions of Jeremy and his favorite toys, how he was just starting to walk and babble baby words, how he liked to be sung to sleep at night and carried through the fields to see the animals. She'd even included a lock of his hair and a print of his hand.

A sennight ago came their reply. To leave them alone and let their son's ghost rest in peace.

So Stephen did the only thing he could. He put Mary and Jeremy into a carriage and brought them across England to the Llewellyns' doorstep. If they were going to refuse to claim their grandson, then damnation, they were going to do it to their faces.

He pounded his fist against the door.

"Stephen," Mary said softly, the first words she'd spoken directly to him since the carriage rolled away from the inn that morning, when she'd called him mad and said that his scheme would come to nothing but sorrow. "We shouldn't do this, not like this. Let's return to the inn and—"

"No." A frontal attack on the enemy worked best with the element of surprise. And he sure as hell couldn't think of a bigger surprise than having their illegitimate grandson arrive unannounced. "We're doing this. If they're going to keep refusing to acknowledge him, then we're going to make them look you in the eyes with their grandson in your arms when they do it."

She bit her bottom lip in a fit of dread, which he ignored. Because of Faith.

In the month since he'd last seen her, the hollowness inside his chest had grown unbearable. He hadn't been sleeping well, had no appetite, couldn't concentrate on running the marquessate...couldn't ride his horse out on the estate for fear he'd turn the animal toward Hartsfield Park. And for all the letters he'd posted to the Llewellyns, he couldn't send a single one to Faith. Her parents wouldn't have allowed it after the way he'd last left Hartsfield.

The only solace he'd found was in the relentless pursuit to help Mary and Jeremy. Which was why they were here. He was tired of waiting. The time had come to force a resolution.

The Llewellyns weren't bad people. Stephen had known them well from his friendship with Daniel, first at Harrow and then at university, and he'd once even spent a short holiday here. He remembered them as loving and friendly, dedicated to hard work and to each other...But he had no idea what the past two years spent mourning their only son had done to them. He hoped their grief hadn't hardened their hearts completely.

The door opened, and the man who served as both butler and footman to the small household nodded politely.

"Yes?"

"Stephen Crenshaw, Marquess of Dunwich, to see Sir Geoffrey and Lady Llewellyn."

The man stiffened as he recognized his name. "Yes, your lordship." His gaze darted to Mary. "And you, ma'am?"

"My companion," he answered brusquely, offering nothing more. He knew without having to look that Mary most likely rolled her eyes in exasperation, thinking him on a fool's errand. "We'll wait to see them."

"Yes, sir." The man looked flustered at the quiet order as he stepped back to let them pass into the house. "Right this way."

"You are shameful," Mary scolded in a low voice after the servant led them to the parlor, then took their coats and hats. "Using your title to barge in like that."

"It might as well be useful for something," he grumbled.

Ignoring his sarcasm, she set Jeremy down on the settee and began to remove his little coat and hat. After four days in the confines of the carriage and small inn rooms at night, the boy fussed restlessly to be put down to explore the large parlor on teetering legs. "I feel like we're ambushing them. And showing up like this without invitation or announcement, when they've already told us to leave them be...You're going to get us tossed out on our ears."

"Whatever it takes, Mary," he muttered and meant it. Feeling just as restless as the boy, he began to pace.

She withdrew a stuffed toy lamb from the pocket of her pelisse and wiggled it in front of Jeremy. "And when this doesn't work, when they refuse us to our faces?" She placed the lamb in the toddler's outstretched hands. "What then?"

"I don't know." But he knew for certain that he wouldn't give up, because the alternative...Well, there was *no* alternative.

Mary sat next to Jeremy, and the boy crawled into her arms, then turned to sit in her lap, the little wool-covered toy still firmly in his hands. He lifted it to his mouth and began to chew on its leather ear. When she looked down at her son, love lit her face.

As he watched them, a longing pierced Stephen so fiercely that he caught his breath. He wanted that same closeness with a family of his own. With Faith. But he wouldn't have any of it unless he convinced the Llewellyns to accept Mary and Jeremy into their lives. Everything depended upon this meeting.

"I suppose we could hold out hope about my parents." She took the lamb from Jeremy and rubbed it against his belly until he laughed. "Of course, it's too soon to hear back from India."

That caught his attention. Stephen wheeled to face

her. "You wrote to your parents?"

The smile on her face faded, and she placed the lamb in Jeremy's lap. "So much time has passed, so much has happened...I decided that the moment was right to try to make amends."

His chest tightened with sympathy for her. The estranged relationship with her parents over Daniel and Jeremy had devastated her, and because she'd been forced to leave India before she was showing with child, she hadn't been able to heal the breech between them. He was glad that she had reached a point where she felt secure enough to contact them, but he prayed her hopefulness wouldn't be dashed.

"Then I hope you hear from them soon," he told her quietly.

"No matter if I don't, because I've decided that I'm going to keep writing to them regardless of what reply I receive. Or don't." She smiled up at him. "Siege warfare."

He quirked a brow. "Oh?"

"I'm going to wear them down until they accept me again, flaws and all." She placed a kiss on the top of Jeremy's head. "Child and all."

Her plotting earned a grudging admiration from him and a smile. The army was looking in the wrong place for strategy experts. They should have been prowling for recruits over tea services in dressmakers' shops.

"Which, I suppose, is the exact same thing you've planned for the Llewellyns, to wear them down until they give in." She cast him a dubious glance. "If they refuse us today, are we encamping in their rose garden?"

His lips pressed together tightly. "I'm glad you find this amusing."

"I don't," she answered quietly. "Not at all."

"Everything will work out," he assured her. If he said it often enough, perhaps he would believe it.

"And you?" she asked softly, a touch of concern in her voice. "Will everything be all right with you?"

"Of course it will." It *had* to. Because living without Faith...impossible. "I'm fine."

With a soft sigh, she shook her head. "I know you, Stephen, and you are the furthest thing from fine. You haven't been yourself since Lady Faith departed Elmhurst Park."

His heart jumped into his throat at her mention of Faith. "It's nothing for you to be concerned with," he answered and turned away to pace again, hoping she would let the subject drop. The last person he wanted to discuss right then was Faith. Not when his future with her depended upon how the next few minutes went with the Llewellyns.

"It concerns *you*, so of course it concerns me because I

care about you," she returned. "She means a great deal to you, I can see it."

"Of course she does. As does all her family," he prevaricated. "We're friends."

"Oh, you're so much more than that," she lowered her voice knowingly although no one could have overheard them.

His gut clenched at the reminder of spending the night in Faith's arms. Which was the very last thing he wanted to think about today. "I don't know what—"

"You *love* her." She smiled gently as she proved her point by commenting, "Only a man in love would be in such distress."

"I'm not in distress," he dissembled, running a frustrated hand through his hair. What he felt was a great deal worse.

Clearly, she didn't believe him, based on her frowning look of disapproval. The same one she gave Polly whenever the young maid tried to sneak into the village to visit the blacksmith's son. "I saw how you two looked at each other."

"You were delusional with fever."

His attempt at teasing only deepened her frown. "You mustn't waste your chance to be with her because of Jeremy and me. Because you feel guilty about Daniel's death."

Halting in his steps, he turned to keep his back toward her so she couldn't see his face. They'd never had this conversation before, about the reasons why he'd pledged his help to her nearly two years ago. They both knew, but neither had voiced it openly. Until now. Fresh guilt and grief clawed at his gut.

Her gaze softened. "You were so very kind to help us when you didn't have to—"

"I did," he ground out, resting a hand on the fireplace mantel.

"No. Daniel's death was not your fault."

He squeezed his eyes shut. Faith had said the same. He would always grieve for Daniel, but now in his heart, he knew he'd made the right decision in ordering his men to charge. He'd come to accept that, thanks to Faith's forgiveness and love. The crushing burden he'd carried since Daniel's death had eased from his conscience, and he could once again look upon his army service with pride, could move forward into the future rather than constantly fight the ghosts of the past. But could anything erase the guilt he felt about Mary and Jeremy?

"You must promise me that no matter what happens today that you will marry her, Stephen. I couldn't bear it if I knew that we were the reason you let her go, that you were unhappy because of us."

He couldn't make that promise. The man he'd been before he left England would have eagerly jumped at the chance to be rid of responsibility and to selfishly have what he wanted, to hell with anyone else. But that man was gone. He knew now the price that hubris exacted, and he was willing to pay it.

He just hadn't expected it to cost him Faith.

"Daniel was the love of my life," she admitted softly as she carried Jeremy across the room to him. "I mourn every day not just for the loss of him but also the loss of the life we would have had together, all the other children we would have had, the home we would have built."

He turned toward her, and the raw pain on her face stole his breath away.

"So many things that other couples take for granted...All those morning walks in the garden that we'll never take, all the quiet evenings sitting by the fireside that we'll never share." A sad smile tugged at her lips. "I would give everything I possess for just one more afternoon spent arguing with Daniel." She swallowed hard, blinking back the tears. "I'll never have that second chance with him. But you, Stephen, you have your second chance, and you must not waste it. So have the happy life together that you both deserve. Please."

He wanted to do exactly that. He wanted to devote the rest of his life to making Faith happy, to laughing with her and making her smile. She deserved a loving home and a family, autumn walks down lanes and midnight picnics, and all the stray animals her heart could love. But he couldn't do it as long as he was responsible for Mary and Jeremy.

He shook his head. "And if the Llewellyns refuse to recognize Jeremy as their grandson, if they refuse to help you?"

"Then you marry her anyway, eloping if you have to," she pressed in a whisper. "Lady Faith is so much stronger than you realize. After all—" She smiled as she tenderly kissed Jeremy's cheek. "—when we're with the people we love, together we can face anything."

"Yes," he rasped out, placing his hand on Jeremy's head and a kiss to her cheek. "You've certainly proved that."

The door opened, and Stephen's heart leapt into his throat. As he drew a deep breath, he turned to face Daniel's parents.

"Dunwich!" Sir Geoffrey stormed angrily into the room, his hands drawn into fists at his side. Behind him, his wife came slowly. Her drawn face paled as her eyes went immediately to Jeremy and locked on the boy.

"Sir," Stephen nodded deferentially to the man although he far outranked him. "I apologize for arriving without notice—"

"You have no right to be here, no right to come into my home like this—" He angrily choked off his words as he jabbed his finger at Mary as she clutched Jeremy to her. "With *them*."

Oblivious to her husband's distress, Lady Llewellyn stepped slowly toward Mary, her attention rapt on the boy.

"You refused to answer my letters and declined an invitation to Elmhurst Park," Stephen reminded him. "You left me with no choice."

"My son is dead because of you!" he cried.

The words pierced him like a knife straight into the heart. He accepted the man's anger without reacting, holding his face inscrutable despite the pain. He'd lived with the overwhelming grief of his best friend's death for the past two years, and he understood the gaping hole that Daniel's absence tore into all their lives. But he hadn't been prepared for the full force of the blame Daniel's parents placed squarely on his shoulders.

Yet he knew the anger only came because they were in pain and needed someone to blame, and he would gladly accept that burden, if it made dealing with his son's death easier. If it made them willing to accept Mary and Jeremy.

Geoffrey's face twisted with grief. "And now you bring that woman into my home, with her lies and schemes to swindle us out of money and ruin Daniel's reputation."

"So you can meet her," Stephen corrected gently, "and meet your grandson."

"That boy is *not* Daniel's!"

At his shout, Jeremy let out a loud wail and began to cry. Mary rocked him in her arms, cooing to him softly, but the boy felt the palpable tension in the room and refused to be calmed.

Lady Llewellyn's face melted with into a heartrending expression of grief and love as she stopped in front of Mary. She whispered, "My God...he looks exactly like Daniel when he was a baby."

She held out her trembling arms in a silent plea.

Mary hesitated a moment, her gaze flicking uncertainly to Stephen. When he nodded reassuringly, she placed Jeremy into the woman's arms. As Lady Llewellyn pressed the boy tightly against her bosom, her own tears began to fall.

"Elizabeth, hand that boy back," Sir Geoffrey ordered, but his voice wavered, and for the first time, Stephen heard the grief underlying the man's anger.

"He's Daniel's son," she whispered, nuzzling her face against the boy's blond hair.

"He's an illegitimate bastard," his father protested, pain lacing his voice. "There's no proof...no proof at all that Daniel and she...that he's..."

"He's *Daniel's* son," she repeated, turning to meet her husband's gaze over the boy's head. "Look at him! Do you think I wouldn't recognize my own babe in him, the son I nursed at my breast and sang to sleep in his cradle? The son I watched grow into a man?" Her voice choked with a sob. "The same son I sent off to India?"

His shoulders sagged, his eyes glistening, as he pleaded, "Elizabeth..."

"*Enough*...enough grief, enough loss...I want it to end now." She pressed Jeremy tightly against her with one arm, while her other reached for Mary. "I lost my son. I will not lose my grandson as well."

They stared silently at each other in a shared communication that only decades of a loving marriage could create. In that moment, his heart pounding wildly and his chest aching for all of them, Stephen knew that everything was going to be all right.

"Geoffrey," Lady Llewellyn whispered, the grief on her face replaced by a look of love and acceptance, "come meet your grandson."

Chapter Twelve

Hartsfield Park
One Week Later

Stephen dismounted from his horse and tossed the reins to the groom who came trotting up through the cold fall drizzle to meet him. A roll of thunder grumbled overhead, and he cocked a defiant eye toward the gray sky. *Bring your worst.* Because nothing short of a storm born of hell itself could stop him now.

With a steely determination that had kept him going nearly nonstop since he left Mary and Jeremy with the Llewellyns, and the last two days through cold rains and mud, he charged up the front steps and past the flustered butler as he stormed into the house without invitation or announcement.

"Your lordship!" The butler scurried after him, completely out of sorts that he would so rudely enter. Worse, that he would bypass waiting in the drawing room or front hall to be announced and instead charged on through the heart of the house.

But Stephen had no patience for niceties today.

"Strathmore!" he shouted, letting that be enough of an announcement of his arrival.

The butler turned white. "Sir, I must insist—"

"So must I, Gibbs," he interrupted but didn't slow in his stride as he stuck his head inside the passing rooms, to search each one before moving on. If he had his way, the butler, the rest of the staff—for that matter, the entire Westover household and family—had better get used to having him prowling their halls. Because he planned on doing just that, for a very long time to come.

Only when he reached the study did he falter, his heart leaping into his throat at finding Strathmore sitting there behind his massive desk. He ignored the rush of blood through his ears, just as he ignored the butler's frantic attempts to make him stop, and took a deep breath to fix his courage.

"Strathmore." Stephen strode up to the duke with the confidence of a man who knew his destiny and wasn't afraid to seize it...or with the grim resolve of a man marching to his own execution. Based on the icy reception that the duke gave him, he wasn't certain which.

Refusing to stand to greet him, Edward Westover

narrowed his eyes on him. "Dunwich."

Stephen removed the small, closed basket he'd worn on a strap around his shoulder all the way from Elmhurst Park and set it on the corner of the desk. Strathmore said nothing, but his eyes darted suspiciously to the basket when it moved.

Stephen tossed his wet hat to the butler, whose mouth fell open at his audacity. "Sir!"

Waving Gibbs out of the room before the man could have a fit of apoplexy right there on the Turkish rug, Strathmore clenched his jaw as he leaned back in his chair and pinned his hard gaze on Stephen. "Is there a reason you've invaded my home?"

"I want to talk to you, sir." He withdrew a bottle of cognac from beneath his caped riding coat and set it in the middle of the desk. "Man to man."

*****

"Poor little thing," Faith whispered.

She reached a trembling hand over the stall door toward the foal. But it was too upset to let her comfort it and continued to pace anxiously around the stall, calling out in distressed bleats for the dam from which it was being weaned.

Tears welled in her eyes and turned the foal into a black blur. She feared for a moment that she might start crying again.

Again? She nearly laughed. When had she *stopped?*

She pulled her wrap tighter around her shoulders against the dreary day and the drip of drizzling rain across the roof. Soon, she would have to return to the house and dress for dinner, plaster a smile on her face for her family, and somehow pretend that her heart wasn't breaking. Her family had all been very kind to her; even her sisters had been surprisingly supportive. Yet each time she had to face them, each time she had to pretend that she was feeling fine when she was nothing but a bundle of raw nerves, with each passing day more certain than ever that she'd made a mistake in agreeing to let Stephen wage an assault on Mary's behalf...*Oh heavens,* how could she continue to bear it?

A tear slipped down her cheek. She couldn't find the strength to wipe it away.

For the past month, since the moment the carriage rolled away from Elmhurst Park and she'd left Stephen behind, she'd been in near-constant sobs. Not sleeping, not eating, going through the days in an anguished fog...Only caring for the animals gave her any comfort, but even that wasn't enough to make her forget the joy she'd found in Stephen's arms that night and the utter wretchedness that consumed her the next morning. The old pain of losing him consumed her, the same anguish and grief that had nearly destroyed her four years ago.

But this time—oh this time it was so much worse! Because she'd tasted love and knew for certain exactly what she was being denied.

His silence was maddening, his absence in her life unbearable. He'd told her that they would only be apart for a few weeks, but a month had passed without any contact from him. After the incident in the stable, Papa had forbidden him to visit Hartsfield or to write to her. Two days ago, unable to bear it any longer, she'd secretly sent a messenger to Elmhurst Park, only to discover from Mrs. Olsen that Stephen had left a fortnight ago, without explanation. Without leaving so much as a note behind for her. And now she was at a complete loss, not knowing what to do except wait, trust in him, and try to keep from breaking down completely.

"There, there...it will all be all right," she spoke gently to the foal in a choking whisper, in an attempt to also comfort herself. "It will hurt for just a little while, then everything will be better."

The faint sound of thunder rumbled overhead, and she pulled her shawl tighter around her shoulders. At least the weather was on her side. A foul and damp day to match her foul and glum mood. And she was glad for it. She didn't think she could have borne sunshine and blue skies—

"Faith."

She wheeled around, her body flashing numb with stunned surprise. "Stephen?"

She stared at him, not daring to believe that she wasn't dreaming, that he truly was here and coming slowly toward her through the stable. Her hand flew up to her chest, as if to physically restrain the thunderous pounding of her heart.

He stopped a few yards from her and set at his feet a small lidded basket he'd been carrying. Then, without a word, his eyes softening with love, he held open his arms.

A soft sob tore from her. She ran to him, rushed into his arms, and threw her arms around his shoulders. She buried her face against his neck as she cried, unable to stop the flood of emotion pouring through her.

The sudden assault on her senses was overwhelming. The familiar scent of him permeated the air around him like the crackle of electricity, and the warm strength of his arms encircling her seeped into her until her stomach fluttered with joy. He was finally here, in her arms where he belonged. He'd come back for her, and she could do nothing but cling to him and sob as happiness swelled inside her.

"Don't cry, my love," he murmured hoarsely into her

hair, his head bowed over hers and his arms tightening their hold around her. "Everything is going to be all right."

"You were gone so long," she whispered. Her hands twisted in the lapels of his coat so thoroughly as to never be able to release him. "I didn't think you were ever going to come for me."

"I'm sorry." His arms tightened around her, as if he were afraid that he'd lose her even now as she stood in his arms, clinging desperately to him. "I came as soon as I could, darling, I promise you that."

The pain of the past few weeks went too deep to release so quickly, and she was unable to stop the hot tears that poured from her and soaked into his neck cloth. "When I'd learned that you'd left Elmhurst Park, I thought—" The words choked in her throat. Taking a deep breath, she tried again, finally daring to voice the fear that had tortured her for the past month. "I thought that you'd given up on us."

"Never." He cupped her face in his hands, and not caring if anyone saw them, he kissed her slowly, deeply, thoroughly. Like a starving man who needed to feast on her lips to survive.

Leaning into him, she eagerly returned the kiss. Her eyes closed, and the sweet sensation carried her away until all she knew was the warmth and strength of him pressing her close, the caresses of his fingers possessively kneading her nape, the love that radiated from him. He was hers, finally and forever. She could barely comprehend all that realization meant, all the love and desire she carried for him.

When she finally tore her mouth away, to regain the breath he'd claimed, she relaxed against him with a shuddering sigh that swelled up from her core. She belonged right here, holding him like this in his arms, and the last tendrils of fear and worry eased from her.

"And Mary?" she asked, half-afraid of the answer. "How is she?"

"Fine. Safe. With the Llewellyns." His lips brushed against her temple with each word. "They've agreed to let her stay, to get to know her and Jeremy."

"Oh thank God," she whispered.

She felt his mouth smile against her forehead. "I have a gift for you," he told her softly. "An apology of sorts for making you worry."

An apology...when she only wanted his heart. She shook her head, smiling up at him through her tears. "I don't need anything now that you're here."

He shook his head. "I left you four years ago because I was a damned fool." His handsome face blurred beneath her tears, but the regret she saw there was unmistakable. "And I had to leave you again these past few weeks in order to make certain that our future together could be a happy one." He reached down to pick up the wicker basket and held it out to her. "But I promise you that I will never leave you again."

Her breath caught in her throat, and she hesitated to accept it. Everything she'd dreamt about was finally becoming hers, and she could barely absorb it all.

"Go on, open it," he urged gently. "I brought it all the way from Elmhurst Park, and the blasted thing nearly killed me," he explained enigmatically with a soft grimace. "The least you can do is accept it so that I don't have to die on the way home."

What on earth...? Her curiosity got the better of her. Slowly, she opened the basket.

A tiny ball of snarling white fur hissed at her as a small paw of bared claws swiped in the air.

Faith blinked. "A kitten?"

"A man-eating beast," he corrected, his mouth hardening into a tight grimace. "Scratched the devil out of me putting it into that basket."

"Of course it did! The poor thing is terrified." Another round of hissing and swiping of claws in a fierce display of bravado went up from the basket. Faith grabbed the kitten by the scruff of its neck and held it up. "Hush now."

It went still and let out a plaintive mewling that melted Faith's heart. She pulled it into her arms and cuddled it against her chest, and the kitten curled into a little ball as it began to purr. Then it looked up at Stephen and let out a fierce hiss for good measure.

"In case that didn't explain it," he drawled drolly, "the little beast is a female."

"Of course she is." With a smile, Faith rubbed her cheek against the kitten's soft fur. "She's beautiful."

"Just like you," he murmured.

Her heart skipped. "And fierce."

"Just like you," he repeated, his eyes shining with pride and love.

Her vision blurred with fresh tears. When the kitten wiggled in her arms, she set it on the ground. It scrambled forward and sank its teeth into Stephen's boot. He stared down at it, his lips pressed into a tight line, saying nothing.

Ruefully, Faith gently pulled it away from his boot and sent it scooting in the other direction. It raced down the aisle as if it owned the place, pausing to hiss and swipe its paw at every horse who poked its head out of its stall to investigate it.

She shook her head. "Charlie the dog is not going to like this!"

"He's just going to have to get used to the idea of sharing you," he murmured, slipping an arm around her waist.

She continued to watch the kitten as it scampered

through the stable. He'd brought her a kitten in apology—*unbelievable*. And so typical of him, to know exactly what would melt her defenses. What would appeal most to her heart. But then, hadn't he always been the man who knew her better than anyone else in the world, even four years apart and two continents away?

Keeping tears of happiness from falling through sheer will, she breathed, "Apology accepted."

His shoulders sagged with relief. "Good. Because there's something else for you inside the basket."

She shook her head. "I don't need any more gifts." She had his love. She needed nothing else.

"This isn't a gift," he corrected quietly. "It's a promise."

He held the basket toward her.

Hesitatingly, she reached inside it again. She half-expected a collar for Charlie or some other such trinket for the kitten, but her fingers brushed against something tiny and metal lying on the satin lining.

She froze, stunned. She couldn't think, couldn't breathe— "Stephen..."

Smiling at her reaction, he reached into the basket and withdrew the ring. The diamond glittered even in the dim shadows of the rain-dreary day.

"I love you, Faith." Dropping the basket to the floor,

he reached for her trembling hand and slipped it onto her finger. "And this ring is a promise from my heart to yours that I will never leave you again, that we will be together, now and always."

He lifted her hand to his mouth and caressed his lips across the ring, then turned her hand over and placed a delicate kiss against her palm.

"Our marriage won't be easy. Mary and Jeremy are with Daniel's parents now, but there will always be rumors swirling about them, about me and my past." He drew a deep breath. "But if you're strong enough to love me, despite all that, then I want nothing more than to marry you, to make a family and future with you."

She sobbed softly when he touched his lips to hers in a kiss so tender, filled with so much love that it tore her breath away.

He knelt on one knee and took her hands in his. "Will you marry me, Faith?"

Before she could answer, the kitten raced back and bit at his boot again with a snarl. Despite her tears, a bubble of laughter rose on her lips at his chagrinned expression as he slid a narrowed gaze down at the ball of fur.

Ignoring the kitten's fierce snarls as it continued to attack his boot, he pressed on, "Marry me, my Faith. Say you'll give me a second chance—"

"Third," she corrected as she swiped at her tears. "But who's counting?"

A slow grin spread across his face as he rose to his feet and slipped his arms around her waist. "I don't deserve you."

She smiled, happiness swelling inside her. "Yet you have me anyway." Then she wrapped her arms around his neck. "You know what everyone will say," she warned teasingly, smiling as her cheek rested lovingly against his. "That you married me because it was expected."

"With you, darling, I will gladly do the expected." He lowered his head and kissed her.

Epilogue

Elmhurst Park

One Happy Year Later

"There you are!" Faith glided into the study with Charlie the dog as ever at her heels and Snowflake the cat nestled in her arms.

Stephen glanced up and smiled at the sight of her and her animal entourage.

They'd been married for almost a year, yet he hadn't grown tired of seeing her beautiful face during long afternoons when he was working at overseeing the marquessate or going over whatever new matter in parliament needed his attention. And he doubted he ever would. Not Faith. Not the woman who brought him more happiness than he could ever have imagined. Just as he'd never grow tired of seeing that same beautiful face filled with pleasure when he made love to her.

He set down the letter he'd been reading, one from

Mary assuring him that she and Jeremy were doing wonderfully well with the Llewellyns, that they'd fully accepted her and legally acknowledged Jeremy as their grandson. They adored the child, and they loved Mary as a daughter. Everything had worked out perfectly in the end.

He pushed himself to his feet and circled the desk toward Faith. When he lowered his head to give her a kiss, the cat hissed and swiped a paw at his chin.

"That's enough from you," he chastised and risked another scratch by setting the beast on the floor.

The animal, which had grown during the past year from a snarling kitten into a snarling cat, gave his boot an indignant bite before turning on Charlie and chasing the cowardly wolfhound into the hall.

"Now then." He slipped his arms around her waist and drew her against him. Her heart jumped into a fast beat, and he grinned at her eager arousal. "You were looking for me?"

"I was." Her arms encircled his neck. "And I'm glad I found you."

"Me, too." He lowered his mouth to her ear and brushed his hands up her sides as he rakishly murmured, "So why don't you forgo whatever plans you have and join me in bed for the rest of the afternoon?"

She sighed. "Oh, that is so tempting..."

Stilling his hands in mid-caress, he raised his head to gaze down into her face and prompted knowingly, "But?"

"Something has come up." She bit her bottom lip with a wary expression. "I'm needed in the stables."

"I see." He released her and leaned back against the desk, folding his arms across his chest before he grabbed her into his arms and carried her upstairs anyway, drama in the stables be damned. "What is it this time?"

She lowered her guilty gaze to the floor. "A cow."

"A *cow?*" he blurted out. Well, *that* was new. Since they'd been married, she'd brought home nearly a dozen stray cats and dogs, two geese, and a rooster. Apparently, though, today she'd graduated to herd animals. Strathmore was certain to have a good laugh over this, now that her kind-hearted rescues had become Stephen's headache.

"It was tangled in the reeds in the river, and the men helped me rescue it. The poor thing was so exhausted from struggling to free itself that I couldn't just leave it there in the field."

He arched a brow. "Cows live in fields."

She wisely ignored his grumbling. "So they brought it back to our stables—"

"They?"

"*I* brought it back," she amended with a sigh. "I want to care for it until I find its owner. Only until then. After all, it has to belong to one of our tenants."

His eyes narrowed suspiciously, knowing her too well. "What aren't you telling me?"

She ground her toe into the rug, refusing to look up at him. "Well, there's a little...you see...just a little..." She hesitated, then admitted in a rush, "It has a calf."

"Of course it does," he mumbled.

"Two of them, actually."

He fought back a grin. Dear God, how much he loved her! "I suppose we'll just have to make room for another mouth to feed," he capitulated. "Or three."

Beaming a grateful smile, she threw herself into his arms with a soft laugh. Then she whispered into his ear, "Or four."

"*Four?*" he blurted out. "Good Lord, Faith! What else did you bring home?"

"I didn't." She pulled back just far enough to look up into his eyes, her gaze shyly hidden beneath lowered lashes. "At least, not yet. Not for another seven months."

Confusion swirled through him. "What do you mean? If you haven't found another stray to bring home, then...then..."

His eyes widened as the realization of what she was saying sank through him. She smiled up at him, an expression of such pure joy on her beautiful face that she glowed.

He whispered, unable to find his voice, "A baby?"

She nodded, her eyes glistening with happiness. "I'm increasing."

Letting out a shout, he grabbed her into his arms and swung her around in a circle, then kissed her with all the love and joy bursting from inside him. A *baby*...He was going to be a father! At last, he would have everything his heart desired, and all because of Faith.

When he sank into the chair and pulled her down across his lap, she twined her arms around his neck. Her fingertips traced lovingly through the hair at his nape as she smiled at him.

"I love you, darling," he whispered. Then he placed his palm against her belly, although it was still as flat as ever. "And I'm going to love this baby, and all the others we'll have."

"*All* the others?" she squeaked out.

He gave her a grinning wink. "Well, we've got to keep up with the cows."

With a happy laugh, she nuzzled her lips against his neck. Then she rested her cheek lovingly against his.

"Why did you never give up on me?" she asked softly. "Even when I'd given up and resigned myself to a life without you, you came back and fought for us, for the happiness and future we could have together."

He folded his arms around her and held her so close that he could feel her heartbeat pounding against his. Every joined beat of their hearts declared their love for each other. And now for their child. "Because I had faith."

"You certainly did," she agreed in a breathless whisper. "And you always will."

Discover More
by Anna Harrington

The Secret Life of Scoundrels Series
Dukes Are Forever
Along Came a Rogue
How I Married a Marquess
Once a Scoundrel

Capturing the Carlisles Series
If the Duke Demands

About the Author

I fell in love with historical romances and all things Regency—and especially all those dashing Regency heroes—while living in England, where I spent most of my time studying the Romantic poets, reading Jane Austen, and getting lost all over the English countryside. I love the period's rich history and find that all those rules of etiquette and propriety can be worked to the heroine's advantage…if she's daring enough to seize her dreams.

I am an avid traveler and have enjoyed visiting schools and volunteering with children's organizations in Peru, Ecuador, Thailand, and Mexico, and I have amassed thousands of photos I unleash on unsuspecting friends who dare to ask about my travels.

I love to be outdoors! I've been hiking in Alaska, the Andes, and the Alps, and I love whitewater rafting (when I don't fall in!). I earned my pilot's license at Chicago Midway (To all the controllers in Chicago Center—I greatly apologize for every problem I caused for you and Southwest Airlines), and it is my dream to one-day fly in a hot-air balloon over Africa.

I adore all things chocolate, ice cream of any flavor, and Kona coffee by the gallon. A *Doctor Who* fanatic (everyone says my house *is* bigger on the inside), I am a terrible cook who hopes to one day use my oven for something other than shoe storage. When I'm not writing, I like to spend my time trying not to kill the innocent rose bushes in my garden.

http://www.annaharringtonbooks.com/
https://twitter.com/aharrington2875

Made in the USA
Columbia, SC
02 January 2019